FALL TWICE

A Small Town Holiday Novella

EVEY LYON

ABOUT

When Lena rekindles a friendship with a former flame, it leads to a healing revelation during her favorite season.

It was supposed to be one coffee. That's what you do when you're a divorced mom and decide to message an old college fling. But Reid is now the professor that people say is irresistible and he lives in the town that by chance I am moving to (found out after the fact, I swear!). Besides, I locked and buried my feelings for Reid long ago. So, it only makes sense to catch up over pumpkin-spiced lattes, and by the time the barista kicks us out at closing, we realize we both could use a friend right now - each other.

But the spark inside me should have been my warning.

Our encounters remind me of another time, and the attraction between us lingers in the air. It doesn't take long before the dear professor is skipping grading papers in favor of me in his bed. But I have reasons to guard my heart, and for once I'm the one in control of our dynamic. And somewhere during the changing season, we ponder the idea that maybe, in life, we are meant to fall in love twice…

Fall Twice is a second-chance novella that celebrates the season of change, Autumn. It will give you all the feels with a dose of steam. Ideal for lovers of pumpkins, single-parent romance, and sexy professors.

LENA AND REID'S PLAYLIST

1. Around Again by Hovvdy
2. You & I by Rhodes
3. I Love That Sound by Michael Bernard Fitzgerald
4. Halloween by Novo Amor
5. Past in Present by Feist
6. Gold Soundz by Pavement
7. Right Where You Left Me by Taylor Swift
8. Airplanes by Local Natives
9. Lay Me Down by The Boxer Rebellion
10. Fake Empire by The National
11. How to Dream by Sam Phillips
12. Hold On When You Get Love And Let Go When You Give It by Stars

LENA

My thumb lingers over the search bar. I'm debating if I should type the letters that will fulfill my curiosity.

Shaking my head, I decide against it and toss my phone to the side and flop on the bed as I blow out a long breath. Leaning to the side table, I grab my wine glass and the bottle to pour another dose of the crisp white liquid. It pairs well with my outfit, as I'm sitting here with my long brown hair in a messy bun, yoga pants, and a t-shirt that says, *Hold on. Let me overthink this*. I think it's pretty fitting to my current situation.

Because that's what I, Lena Gold, do on a daily basis. Overthink.

This is not exactly how I thought my life would pan out at age thirty-two.

It was supposed to be a life of marriage, kids, and hopefully a dog behind a white picket fence. But somewhere over the years, the dream in my grasp slowly trickled through my fingers. The marriage is now over, our calendars are now synchronized to plan when we each get to see our son, and here I am moving halfway across the country.

Oscar, my six-year-old son, is with his father for the next week while I sort out finding a house and other logistics for our move to a new town. Sighing, I realize how lucky I am that the divorce was… peaceful.

We have good communication and continue life the way we were married, as friends. That's what happened. Something was missing and only that. We were a good team otherwise, more like glorified roommates than lovers. Now, Sean is soon moving to Tokyo for a six-month assignment to further his career, and I'm moving to Hollows, Illinois, the place where I have a shiny new job nearby.

Bye-bye, Maryland.

After a decent sip of Chardonnay, I swap the drink for my phone again. I'm beginning to wonder if it's my subconscious giving me a nudge. Quickly, I check that my flight to Chicago tomorrow is still on schedule before I hop onto social media to scroll through friends' feeds, filled with avocado toasts, island holidays, first birthdays, and an adorable puppy playing in the changing September leaves. Damn, to think there was a time in my life when social media wasn't even a thing.

I stop scrolling when I come across a guy who I once went on two dates with. I scoff a laugh because yikes, that was a disaster. I was twenty and clueless. Why are we still connected via social channels?

Because I believe that unless they are a cheater, did something awful, or were simply born an ass, then we didn't work out for a reason. And because of that, it led me to other paths, and those roads led me to the guy I married, and that guy and I created the best kid in the universe. Everything led me to my son. And yes, it's a cliché, but the moment he was placed in my arms then it all made sense.

This is why I find myself staring at another ex's post on my feed—my first real boyfriend when I was sixteen—and he's holding his newborn child. See? We weren't meant to be, and because of that, he is now with his wife of eight years and has three kids. It's not that crazy. It's not like we message on a weekly or even yearly basis. It's more that we monitor one another's lives at random times.

I tilt my head to the side as I contemplate if this really is a good idea, running down the list of exes.

But what the hell, right?

Scrolling, I stop on the lawyer I dated when I was twenty-four, and I'm relieved it didn't work out, as he is now traveling the world, and it looks like commitment hasn't crossed his mind. Or at least his photo of scuba diving gives me that vibe.

Then there is the guitar guy who I had a summer fling with once. Based on his likes and photos of warrior poses, then my guess is he seems to be one of those yoga guru types of people now.

My thumb begins to type a name in the search bar, but I stall.

I've been doing this all night. Because there is one name that still causes a blip inside of me.

The guy that throughout the years, at random times, we would send a *hey* or *happy holidays,* and I don't think it was just to be polite either, it was pure genuine curiosity. Reid must be married now, or at least last time we messaged he was engaged.

It was surprising when my friend, Annie, mentioned she heard a rumor that Reid was in Chicago, and that's how I ended up with my thumb dancing in a waltz with the internet search bar for the last few hours.

I finally hit enter and Reid Stone pops up on my screen. He hasn't updated his profile in a *long* time. But make no mistake, that photo from two years ago is 100% Reid. Brown hair relatively short but with a wave, and brown eyes that hold you with a glance, and now he is sporting a stubbled sharp jawline, with his smile still easy and naturally warming with a dose of sin. I see he hasn't ditched the casual blazers either.

Biting my bottom lip, I feel my eyebrow raise when I see that he's living in Hollows. The place where I am moving to. Of all the Chicago suburb options, he ended up there.

My entire body straightens from surprise. Up until earlier today, the last I heard he was teaching in Georgia at some small liberal arts college. I sink back onto my pillows when I remind myself that he's married and our fling in college was just that, nothing more.

I bet he's doing well in life. But what a coincidence, an odd chance.

Opening my chat history, I see our last interaction was a few years ago when he congratulated me on my son's third birthday because I had posted a photo. It was a short message

Congrats on the b-day, he looks cute. You look happy.

To which I replied, **Thanks, hope you are well. I see you're engaged, happy you found someone.**

Internally I'm impressed someone managed to tie him down, and I mean that figuratively and in the completely inappropriate literal way. Debating for only a second, I remind myself of my solid philosophy. Every road led me to my son. It all happened for a reason. This is exactly why I type out a message and hit send.

Me: Hey! Long time. Hope you are well. Not sure you

even check this anymore. This is kind of crazy, but I noticed you're in Hollows, and I am going to be in town for a few days. If you want to catch up, then let me know.

I throw my phone to the side. That was easy enough. I slide off the bed and look at the boxes that are accumulating in the house. Sean already moved out to a temporary apartment a while back while we waited for the house to sell, and I need to be out within three weeks.

I decide to get to work on the books on the shelf in the bedroom, since they're the simplest to pack.

But when my phone pings, I look at the screen to see that Reid responded.

Reid: Yeah, I'm in Hollows. Moved here two years ago when I got tenure. Small world, I guess. We should meet up.

A smile tugs on my lips and I'm quick to type back.

Me: Cool. I get in tomorrow, but probably will be beat. Perhaps Tuesday?

Reid: Sure. 4?

Me: That works. Just send me the address of where you want to meet. I'm not too familiar with the area.

Reid: Okay. Is your kiddo with you?

Me: No. I'm in town for business.

I figure I should leave out that I'm divorced, packing up my life, and moving there. It's more of a second cup-of-coffee discussion. Don't want to sound too stalkerish right off the bat.

Reid: There's a coffee spot. They have tea since you don't drink coffee.

My body stills because he remembers the small details. In college, I never drank coffee, only green tea.

Me: I drink coffee now.

He sends me an impressed emoji.

Reid: Well then, I'll see you at Ginger & Co.
Me: Okay.

Closing the chat, I pause with the phone resting against my chin. Gosh, it's been ten years since I saw him, and our lives sure have changed. All the more reason that I'm not sure why there is something resembling excitement floating inside of me.

A knock on the inner pane of the bedroom door breaks my thoughts. Looking up, I see Annie, my best friend. She went to collect dinner after helping me pack a few boxes. Annie and I went to college together and then parted ways, and by chance her career brought her here a few years ago which allowed us to reconnect.

She greets me with a smile, her blonde hair pulled into a tight ponytail. "You okay? You look lost."

I nod. "Completely." I walk to the open box and dump in a few books. "Did you bring some takeout?"

"Yep, Chinese is here. I was calling you from downstairs, but you didn't answer."

"Come on, I'm starving." I push the box to the side with my foot, and I turn to Annie to walk with her back downstairs.

"All ready for house hunting and school registration?" she asks as we walk into the kitchen, and she begins to unpack the bag of food.

"As prepared as I can be," I say and grab a few plates.

She slides a carton of noodles in my direction. "Anything else you need for your trip? I'll drop you off at the airport tomorrow. I've decided to thwart my own plan to lock you up so you can't leave me because, as your best friend, I realize that this may be a good change for you." Her hand comes to her heart in a half-sincere and half-joking declaration.

"Thanks." I grin at her because none of this is easy, but I

need a change of scene, and Sean asked his employer if he could be based out of Chicago when he gets back from his assignment.

A forkful of food lands in my mouth. "Mm, this is good." I swallow then casually mention, "He's in Hollows."

She shrugs her shoulders at me as she sharpens her chopsticks like a pro.

"Reid," I clarify.

Her chopsticks fall onto the counter and her eyes go wide. "No way. I thought he moved to Chicago from what I heard, but I didn't think it would be the town where my dear friend just so happens to be moving to."

My mouth goes slack as I try to figure out why her reaction is so dramatic. "It's no big deal. He's a professor now and married, I think."

I hear her hum in doubt. "And you're going to see him?"

I laugh at her dramatic tone. "Sure, why not? We're all adults at different points in our lives."

Annie plants her hands on her hips and she gawks at me. "Except in college, you two were… explosive."

"We were not," I refute. "We are just meeting for coffee."

She rolls her eyes. "Okay. But I want the play-by-play after. I mean, I think I saw an article on him a year or so ago. Easy on the eyes, for sure. Definitely making waves in the academic world."

I focus on my food. "Exactly. All the more reason that it's a simple coffee. He has the life he wants, and I need to focus on this move. I'm not twenty-two anymore, wanting a fuck-buddy who meets me in the library."

She walks to me and places her hand on my shoulder. "I know. It's just… be careful. Fires can reignite."

Confidently, I stand tall. "Really, we are just two people catching up over coffee."

Annie gives me a knowing look, not quite believing my words but willing to play along.

"Of course. But if he orders a pumpkin spiced latte then run."

My face turns amused and puzzled. "Why?"

"Because the Reid I remember doesn't do seasonal drinks, let alone enjoy your favorite time of year. If he orders pumpkin anything then he's changed, and that's your warning."

I shake my head at her logic. "That is the most ridiculous theory, but since I love you then I will take it into consideration."

She smiles in accomplishment.

———

TWO DAYS LATER, I find myself walking down the main street of Hollows, a cute northern suburb of Chicago. It has historic charm, and it's quiet for a weekday but by no means too still. I bet in the next hour it'll get busy when the Metra trains start to deliver people who worked downtown for the day. I spot Ginger & Co.

The glass of the window has white lettering and a sketched piece of ginger against a coffee cup. There's a young couple sitting by the window, but the place looks big. At first glance, I see it's two stories that you can see, as the middle is open, and it has one big wall of books.

Truthfully, I feel something quickening inside of me as I approach the door.

There's a chalkboard on the sidewalk announcing their specials of the month—a ginger turmeric health blast and a spiced apple cake.

Blowing out a breath, I feel excited to catch up with an

old... well, I'm not sure what Reid is. But I'm late, and he must be waiting.

I pull the handle, and I internally remind myself, *Reid doesn't drink pumpkin lattes*.

And I open the door.

L ooking at my laptop screen, I scowl. Emails from students who are trying to justify their late assignment submissions always cause an eye roll. The excuses are either offensive because they didn't put in thought to come up with something more original, or too creative so that it feels unbelievable.

Teaching political history has been my daily grind for the past few years, after working in a non-profit. The academic life called to me, and here I am.

Closing my laptop, I look around Ginger & Co. to see if she's arrived.

Jesus, like a comet coming out of nowhere, I didn't expect to hear from Lena.

She's married now and with a kid. Everything she always wanted. Sure, over the years we would wish one another well. To my surprise, too, considering how things ended between us—a parting of ways as two people who had relied on one another during that final grueling year of college. And now here we are as full-fledged adults.

I place my computer in the bag since I know she will be

here any second. I arrived early to grade assignments, plus this place is my establishment. I frequent this cafe several times a week.

The sound of the door opening causes me to look up, and for the life of me I can't figure out why the next few seconds feel like I'm watching a scene in slow motion, a moment in my life that I will never forget.

She looks exactly the fucking same. Her hair is long and in waves, partly curled, and her eyes, hazel, that I'm sure still change depending on the light. To my astonishment, she's wearing skinny jeans and a deep green turtleneck. Lena always wore dresses and skirts in college, but this look suits her too.

Her eyes flick up and land on me, with her lashes fluttering, the line of her mouth stretched just enough, and her fingers tipped with pale red nails tuck a loose strand of hair behind her ear.

I stand to greet her, and I'm stunned that I can function. Half of my brain feels excited, and the other half warns me this will taunt me about a life I didn't choose.

Lena slows down as she approaches me; a nervous smile plays on her soft pink lips. "Hey, have we met?" She pretends to squint her eyes in confusion.

It causes me to grin. "Unfortunately, we have."

Hug or no hug? This is kind of awkward. I follow her cues, but she is as neutral as the color gray. I hold my arm out to offer a side hug, and we keep it short and loose.

The touch is enough to short-circuit something inside of me, but I choose to ignore it.

After we both land on the comfy lounge chairs, we stare at one another, both in disbelief that we are in front of the real-life versions of one another.

"Lena Gold, it's good to see you," I tell her sincerely.

Her soft smile hasn't faded. "Yeah, kind of unexpected but good nonetheless."

A barista arrives to take our order. Normally, you need to order at the counter, but they know me here.

"Pumpkin spiced latte?" I suggest to Lena, and my hand comes up like I have a good idea.

Her look turns to concern. "Do you drink pumpkin spiced lattes?" She almost seems petrified.

My face turns puzzled. "Of course not." Relief floods her face. "I go for the gingerbread coffee."

Now her eyes go slightly wide, and her mouth parts open, with no words coming out. She shakes her head gently as if she is speaking internally. "Uh, pumpkin spiced latte sounds good."

The barista smiles in response before she leaves.

Sinking back into the chair, I cross my arms and look at Lena. Damn, she hasn't changed except her hair is lighter and maybe she's a little older around the eyes. "When did you start drinking coffee?"

She laughs as she places her sweater to the side. "When I became a mom."

"Yeah, I hear that a lot from colleagues and my sister."

"It isn't a myth, I assure you."

I hold my hands up. "Don't worry, I don't need to be convinced. And what brings you to Hollows?"

She stalls for a second then awkwardly smiles. "Work. I have a new job at Ives & Wells in Chicago, the marketing firm. I'll be working from home mostly."

"That's cool."

Her eyes seem to be assessing me, from head to toe, actually. "You really are going for the professor look, huh?"

I glance down at myself and see my usual dress shoes,

jeans, button-down shirt, and blazer. "This was always my style," I defend.

She tilts her head to the side. "The stubble is a bit more."

The barista arrives with our drinks, and we thank her. Lena and I both take hold of our mugs of coffee.

"Will your wife or fiancée meet us later?" she innocently asks as she stirs a spoon in her mug.

I raise my eyes and run my tongue along the inside of my mouth. "Nah, she's kind of history."

"Oh." Lena looks down at her drink and then back to me. "Sorry, I just kind of assumed since I remember seeing something once. Your social media isn't exactly the source of many clues."

I smirk because she's right. "It's okay, you didn't know. Tamara and I broke up about a year and half ago."

"Weren't you two together for quite a while?"

"Four years, yeah, but she didn't want to get married in the end, so *c'est la vie*." I place my drink on the side table. At that moment, I notice that Lena is missing an accessory that I was expecting on her finger. "You seem to have lost a ring."

She gulps the small cookie that came with the coffee. "That's because I did. I got divorced recently."

My entire body freezes for a second or two as my brain adjusts. I was planning to catch up with Lena, as the guy whose life is gray and her who is very much taken. That expectation now went out the window.

"It's okay," she assures me. "He's off to Tokyo for work soon, and he won't be taking our son with him. Actually, we're on good terms."

I slowly nod in understanding. "Can I ask why it ended?'

"Oh, uhm… maybe I'll fill you in over alcohol sometime," she chortles. "Anyway, I'm actually moving here due to my job. I had no idea you lived here until two days ago, so that was a fun plot twist."

Jesus, what is the universe throwing at me? I haven't been waiting for her, but something about this puts me on edge. "Here?" I point down to the floor. "As in Hollows?"

She sucks her spoon then pulls it out. "Yep." She pops the P. "Good schools and easy commute. That's why I'm here for a few days, to sort out the relocation."

"Right." It comes out faintly from my end. Internally slapping myself, I know I need to not let my thoughts stray. "Your… son?" I remember seeing a photo of her and her son at his birthday on social media, a rare one, as she doesn't post much of him.

Lena smiles because she knows we're both digesting these new facts that we discovered about each other. "Oscar is a star. He just turned six and doesn't seem fazed by this change of situation. I did promise him a turtle or frog, so maybe that plays a role."

I scratch my thumb over my chin. "Amphibians some-times do the trick."

A thick silence overcomes us as we stare at one another. For a moment, I remember another time when we met at party then realized we were in the same political science class together. We became two people who studied together in the library and fucked like crazy at night.

And even though I knew it was a fine line, I let us continue for a year. Never making it official and never giving a promise. We were friends first, or lovers—truthfully, it blurred, but we weren't boyfriend and girlfriend, that's for sure. But God, we cared for one another.

Every now and then I would wonder if she got the life she wanted. I knew she was meant to be a mom and marry a man who wanted to settle down. Back then, I wasn't the guy for her, and she wasn't what I wanted or needed. We weren't even going to stay in the same state. Doesn't mean she didn't linger in my thoughts throughout the years, a constant wonder that I just never understood.

Now she seems lost yet content as she plays with that damn spoon. "September is a good month, October and November even better. I like that this place has a ginger theme." She randomly speaks as if she's trying to fill the shift in our air.

"I remember." I bring my hands behind my head. "You would dance in the leaves."

Our eyes catch, and I notice she swallows. "I did... So, tell me, Mr. Professor, what else have you been up to?"

"Nothing crazy. I taught down in Georgia and here I am now. It's a great university here."

"Not too pretentious?" She raises a brow because for the most part I'm laidback, and I hate anything that resembles the life my parents lead.

"Not unless you have dinner with the dean. Okay..." I clap my hands together. "So you're moving here."

She weaves her fingers through her hair, and I notice the earrings she's wearing are little flower studs. "I am. I looked at a few places today, found a townhouse. I can't deal with a normal house now, the idea of mowing grass after years of never doing it is a tad too much. Plus, the subdivision has a communal playground, gym, and pool. I'm going to sleep on it then probably put a deposit down tomorrow. I need to visit the elementary school to register Oscar, but that's just boring stuff that you don't need to know." She looks away.

"Where are you staying?"

"The inn on the edge of town. I fly back at the end of the week. Where do you live?"

I grin proudly. "I got a great apartment in a historic

building that I'm 100% positive you would say is a cliché professor address, but it fits the bill."

"I'm not going to say it's cliché unless you tell me you drive an old convertible." My face cracks, and she bursts out in laughter when I don't answer. "Oh my God, you really are going all out on this."

I shrug my shoulders. "My dad gave me his old Ferrari, and I love it."

"I can only imagine. You don't have kids and I know you hate pets, so the car works. Your family good?"

"Same old, thanks for asking. Hey, don't you still see Annie?"

Lena smiles brightly. "I do. We live near one another. She's a bit angry that I'm leaving, but she'll visit. She is also in academia, psychology."

"Good."

"How are you, Reid? I mean…" She debates what to say. "It's been years, and I feel like nothing yet everything has changed. What have you been up to the last few years?"

"Enjoying life. Seeing great concerts, exploring the city, collecting bottles of wine. The usual, you know."

She shakes her head at me. "You ordered gingerbread coffee. Something must have changed because in college it was either beer or black coffee. Next, you're going to tell me that you have a tattoo or adopted a cat."

Christ, she sees right through me.

"No cat, or tattoo. Life has just been busy."

She doesn't seem to buy it. "Okay, fair enough. We haven't really spoken in person in ten years, so everything is kind of strange. I mean, here I am just showing up out of the blue telling you that I'm divorced and moving here. Kind of crazy if you think about it."

"You've always been quirky."

Her head falls into her hand. "I just… wow, here we are. I kind of thought I would never see you again."

"Me too." For reasons she doesn't know.

"What does that mean?" She perks her head up.

Honesty with her only feels right.

"I had cancer."

The barista arrives. "Another coffee?"

Lena's face drops and she blinks a few times, and I notice her chest move up and down.

My gaze doesn't part from Lena as I answer the barista. "I think we could use another round, thanks."

Lena's eyes connect with my own, and for the first time in the longest time, I feel like someone won't let go.

3
REID

The new round of coffees is placed in front of us. Lena hasn't said anything, she just looks at me with eyes hazed, and I reach my hand out to touch her arm to reassure her.

"I'm fine now. It's gone."

She clears her throat. "I had no idea."

"Not many people did."

"You could have died." Her voice is emotional.

I smile weakly. "Nah, I'm not that easy to get rid of." A long moment of silence lingers between us. "It was testicular, caught early at a routine check-up, and yeah, I still have my balls intact," I attempt to joke and release my hand, feeling a loss of her warmth against my skin.

Her gaze slides down ever so gently then back up at me. "Chemo?"

I shake my head. "Radiation and a small surgery. Got to keep my hair, froze some sperm. Luck was on my side, just an average sabbatical, really."

"Was this before or after your ex…"

"Before. And if it's any reassurance, that isn't why she

left. We were together for a few months after I was in the clear, it's just she wasn't *in love* with me and felt more of a connection with her new colleague at her firm."

She tips her coffee cup into my direction. "Her loss. And if it's any consolation, my ex-husband and I were more room-mates than anything." Her tongue darts along her lips to taste the brew. "But fuck. Cancer. I honestly, I…" She looks away.

"Relax. It's a thing of the past."

"You could have died," she bites back her reminder again. "I wouldn't have known. I mean, would you have told me if it was bad? Don't people have a list of who they contact, and those lists go way back?" she rambles.

Her tone surprises me slightly, or rather that she would be so affected by it.

I glide my finger along my top lip. "Only a small group knew. I thought about contacting you, and even typed and deleted the message a few times. But luckily, I didn't get to the stage of who to contact in case you die. How about a happier topic?" I attempt to derail this morbid direction of catching up. "Still swim laps? Love cake? Or is there some-thing earth-shattering to tell me?"

She rolls her eyes before she pinches my arm like time hasn't passed. "This is kind of a big deal. But fine, I will play along. No to swimming. I run and knit." She holds her palm up as my mouth gapes open. "I know, I know, a far cry from dancing on tables and downing tequila shots."

I lean back and grin at this news. "Shit, you've calmed down, well, you seem calmer anyway."

"We've only been speaking for a half-hour tops."

"I can see it in your face. You seem… at peace."

She laughs under her breath and crosses one leg over her other. "Trust me, that isn't my mantra as of late. Getting a divorce feels like a death; nobody gets married hoping for a divorce. I'm just past the grieving state, and I have to make this all work, you know? The co-parenting thing, I mean."

"I'm sure you will rock at it, the mom stuff and doing it on your own sometimes. Being a mom is always what you wanted and what you would be good at."

Her eyes narrow. "What makes you say that? We didn't exactly talk about a future when we were…" She waves a hand. "You know."

I lean against a propped elbow on the side of the chair. "Not entirely true. There was that one time when we needed the morning-after pill."

And for some reason, my mind took us there. We had hooked up for the third time and the condom broke, and we were far too relaxed about the situation. Looking back, that was the closest glimmer to creating a family I've ever had.

Lena looks around the coffee shop and back at me. "Wow, you are digging up the archives."

"Considering our history, something was going to come up at some point tonight."

Her head bobs from side to side. "Fair point."

"What made you send me a message?" I wonder.

"Really, it was the coincidence of location. I mean, I thought you had a wife by now. Just felt odd to come here and not say 'oh hey, what's up, Reid?'"

"Say my name again," I request.

"Reid." Her tone is slightly confused.

Wow, my name on her lips is a throwback to a time of hard academics and survival mode to enter the big, bad adult world. Except for those nights and afternoons when we would just lie in bed with music on after I took her in ways that she would let me try.

"It's good to see you again," I admit softly.

Her face stays neutral as she studies me. "Don't lie to me. It's not like I crossed your mind over the years."

"Come on, Lena, I cared for you. It's not like I could ever forget you. By the way, you really should try the carrot cake here," I attempt not to let us linger in the sentimentalism.

"Let me guess, they use ginger," she mundanely retorts.

"You were always so smart." I look into my cup and realize I really don't need any more caffeine right now. "Hollows is right up your alley. It's quaint and they have a fall festival. Thanksgiving was always your thing; well, they celebrate it like four months of the year here. The grocery store down the road has had a display of cornbread mix since the end of August." I throw my thumb over my shoulder.

"Which makes it even more surprising that you're here. Wouldn't you want to live in the big bad city with an option of women?" She folds her arms over her chest as she teases me.

"Nah, I enjoy my coffee in peace these days."

She grins so big that it's almost infectious as her eyes raise to me. "As long as you haven't slept with a student."

I scoff at her suggestion. "Please, I'm not that stupid. But happy to hear your opinions of me are so honorable," I say, sarcastic.

"Okay, okay. I guess we have a lot of years to catch up on," she comments as she touches a bracelet on her wrist.

"Then let's start from the beginning," I suggest, with her eyes landing on my own.

And with time stopping, we both talk about our lives. After graduation, Lena worked in a marketing job that she hated, met her husband at the gym, and followed him to Maryland for his job. Except for Annie, she didn't feel at home there, so she wanted a change. And here she is, because she applied for jobs that would be near where Oscar's father will work when he comes back from Tokyo, and also because Oscar's grandparents from his father live a few hours away and she is still closer to them than her own folks.

Me? I did my PhD and got into teaching. I've lived a few locations, but I've been here for a few years, and my ex is walking somewhere around the state, but I have no contact with her.

Lena's face lights up every time she talks about her son, and she leans in to show me a photo of her little boy. He has the eyes of the woman whose hair smells of macadamia, whose back I'm touching as if I have every right to.

"Then there was this time when I completely went ballistic at the mom at the soccer game. I mean, they were only four and she was acting like they were training for the World Cup." She looks up at me and stops. "Oh, sorry, I'm blabbing about mom stuff. You're not a kid person, I know. Anyway, I swear, I've acquired other skills over the years. I'm a pro at conquering any Ottolenghi recipe or distinguishing cheap white wine from expensive." She's rambling, and my smile doesn't fade.

She notices that I'm just watching her. "You okay?"

Clearing my throat, I straighten up my posture and release my hand from her back, breaking our connection. "Totally."

Lena snorts at my response. "Years may have changed us, but in no universe would you say totally."

Completely right.

I pinch the bridge of my nose. "Okay, you got me. It's just surreal sitting here, you know?"

She touches my thigh in a friendly way. "Yeah, I know." Her voice is nearly delicate.

The barista slowly walks to us with an awkward look. "Sorry, but we kind of need you two to finish up because we're closing."

"Shit," I say and look at my watch. "It's almost eight."

We've been sitting here for hours, just talking about our lives and random things.

Lena grabs her sweater. "Wow, I had no idea of the time. For sure, we'll finish up."

I go and pay the bill, to her protest, and we gather our stuff. Meeting outside, we stand under the streetlight and look at one another.

"Want me to give you a ride?" I offer as I hold up my car key.

She shakes her head. "No, it's okay. I have my rental car."

Something inside of me keeps holding onto this moment; I don't want it to end.

Because in truth, I've been lonely lately. Most of my friends are colleagues who either spend their days on research papers or with their growing families. My own family is a two-hour plane ride away, and I've filled my days with a routine.

But the last few hours, I've come out of a shell that I didn't realize I was in, and if this is what feeling alive is, then I should probably prolong it.

We step toward one another and wrap our arms around each other for a hug, the kind you should have when you reunite with an old friend, and I feel her relax in my hold, even when I hug her tighter.

This moment can't end, but right now it feels like this was the way our night should close.

She gently pulls back. "It was good to see you again."

"Likewise."

Lena steps away, and I know she wants me to lead. "We should stay in touch since we're practically neighbors," I suggest.

"Sounds like a plan."

We both stall, and when she is about to pivot to leave, I don't hold back. "I don't know if you have any plans tomorrow, but I only have a morning lecture. We could grab lunch, or I could help you with any moving logistics." It sounds casual enough, an offer a friend would make.

Her face lifts, and the corners of her mouth twist. "That would be great. Tomorrow then." She turns to walk away but stops and looks over her shoulder at me. "Good night, Reid."

My mouth quirks at her sentimental tone before we finally part ways.

LENA

I slide into the second row of the lecture hall as the busy room gets settled. Reid just entered, but he has no clue I'm here—hazards of the university publishing the class schedules online.

Turns out my morning errands went quicker than planned, and I figured this would be kind of fun. I sip on my to-go cup of tea as I watch the students pull out their tablets and laptops. It may have been a decade ago, but we were more paper notebook kind of people.

I glance down at my phone.

Annie: Should I just hand you the match since you're seeing him again?

I roll my eyes. We spoke last night, and I caught her up. I'm positive it was five minutes before she stopped a slur of continuous *no ways*.

Me: Considering how my year has gone, trust me, that romance is nowhere on my agenda. Especially with Reid.

Annie: I'm going to grab my popcorn.

I turn my phone face down to ignore her.

Reid closes the door, then turns on the PowerPoint

presentation with a little remote as he perches on the edge of the desk like he owns the place. I'm curious how long it will take for him to notice that I'm here unexpectedly. There are about fifty people in the auditorium.

He pushes his blazer to the side as he tucks a hand in his jeans pocket. "Okay, everyone, we're going to get right into it. If you are here today and haven't handed in your assignment due yesterday, then you best believe you are seeing me after class."

A few from the crowd chuckle, and I have to smile to myself. I can picture Reid as relatable to the students, but a complete hard-ass when needed. My eyes blink closed for a second, and I remember sitting in a similar row and the way we would chat before the start of a lecture or how he would look over my shoulder at my notes.

Here he is, the ruler of the kingdom.

This isn't how I predicted my week would go. I didn't expect for him to be single, a survivor, or the guy that feels like a magnet when I'm around him. Nor did I plan for us to see one another again. This morning I woke after the shock had worn off and found instead that relief filled me, that in a way Reid and I have both had a loss, and for that, we can relate to each other more than with other people.

Reid propels off the desk to pace a few steps as he changes slides. "We continue our journey to understand Glasnost at the end of the Cold War." His eyes scan the room, and when he spots me, I flash my eyes. He pauses for a second in his speech and I see the subtle tick of his jaw as if he wants to smile, but he stops himself and continues.

The entire hour, I watch in awe at the way he captivates the room. He knows when to ask questions and invites discussion. By the time the lecture is finished, I can't help but smile at the way Professor Reid is in reality.

I stay put as a group of students approach him, and behind me, I hear two girls speaking in hushed tones. "I fucking hate this topic, but I will literally listen to him talk about rice if it means I can stare at him for an hour," one of the girls mentions, and I try to keep my chuckle from escaping. "I would kill to have him as my thesis advisor and have weekly one-on-ones. I bet we could negotiate some extra credit." The other sighs.

Now, I just shake my head gently to myself. With the room becoming more vacant, I slowly approach the professor as he leans against the desk.

"Professor Stone" I greet him with knowing eyes.

His grin now emerges as he scans the room. "Wasn't expecting you here."

"I know we were going to meet for lunch, but I couldn't resist." I smile as I stand in front of him. "It was too easy, and besides, I hear extra credit could be fun with you." I wink.

He scratches his cheek as he keeps his grin in control. "I don't even want to know."

"You have a fan club." I tilt my head in the direction of the door.

"And you are probably the guest of honor at their meetup this week," he jokes as he packs up his laptop.

I fake shock and fold my arms over my chest. "This is what I get for taking interest in your profession?"

His hand lands on my shoulder. "Come on, I need to get you out of here, otherwise I'll have rumors starting amongst the students. Plus, I'm starving."

"Okay." I turn serious. "But really, it was an interesting hour, and it suits you, teaching, I mean."

"Thanks. If it's any consolation, if I didn't know who you were then I would have assumed you were twenty-one and just another student."

I nudge his arm with my own. "Don't flatter me. Otherwise, I may feel inclined to buy you lunch."

"You know I wouldn't let you anyway, because I'm a gentleman."

"Yes, but I'm not traditional, and we're friends. Plus, you bought coffees last night," I justify.

He ruefully shakes his head and leads the way.

———

REID WATCHES me as I stuff a chili dog into my mouth. I have no qualms about eating like this, it's the best thing in my life right now.

"I wasn't expecting this. You were a salad person, like a straight-up dressing-on-the-side salad person." He chomps into his burger.

I swallow and wipe my mouth with the napkin. "I know, but it's all about balance which I finally figured out. Plus, I've heard stories about this place, and I'm not leaving until we get the chocolate eclair cake."

He salutes me. "Yes, ma'am."

"It must be nice not to have to teach all day. I guess it offsets with grading papers and thesis advising?"

"It does." He doesn't seem interested to talk about work. "So tell me, what is on the agenda for today? Did you pick your place?"

I smile, satisfied with my choice. "I did. I get the keys in two weeks, already booked the movers, and I just need to order a new bed and a few things for Oscar. I don't care if I have to sleep on a box, his room has to be ready when he moves in. I'll come out for a few days first, then his father will bring him here."

I'm surprised by the way he patiently listens every time I go on and on about my son; he almost seems interested.

"I guess we could hit up some stores so you can look at stuff."

I playfully slam my hand down onto the table. "You volunteer to go shopping with me?"

He shrugs. "Why not? Besides, something tells me that you need to be kept in line so you don't veer off track."

A sound escapes from the back of my throat. *Kept in line.* It sends a shiver down my spine in a warm way, never mind the flashback of him pinning me against a wall after a party.

"Offer accepted," I say without thought, knowing I should be more hesitant to the suggestion. "The assistant at my new job offered to help, but I think it kind of feels better to do this stuff with someone I'm more familiar with."

He draws his thumb along the line of his jaw. "You're familiar with me?" He seems amused.

I tilt my head to the side. "I mean, it's been years, but it feels the same and different, if that makes any sense."

He smiles gently. "I get it." He glances outside. "Hey, have you had the grand tour of Hollows yet?"

I shake my head. "Only the windshield tour. Know a good tour guide?" I play along.

"Come on, let's get your cake to-go, and I want to show you something." He stands up abruptly and offers me his hand.

I stare at his hand for a second extra before sliding my own onto his palm because I'm curious where our day will go, yet scared that every time we touch that feeling of complete attachment to someone returns, but I push that thought to the side.

Ten minutes later, we are walking down Main Street, and we head straight to a candle store that has Halloween decorations in the window, but not the kind you find at commercial stores. It's more... classic, chic, or quite possibly authentic.

We walk in and the bell rings over the door, getting hit with the smell of cinnamon and sage instantly.

Reid leans in to speak softly into my ear. "People say she has powers." I hear enough humor in his tone.

A lady in her thirties appears, with dark hair, jeans, and a black t-shirt. "Oh, hi there, Reid, who is this lady you bring by today?"

He scratches the back of his head. "This is Lena, an old friend."

"It's okay, you can say lover. I see the connection between you two, and I don't even need to take out my cards." She smiles calmly.

I chortle a laugh.

Reid just smiles as he looks between us. "Lena, Prudence. Lena here is moving to Hollows and could probably use something for her new place."

Prudence claps her hands together. "Of course. Need something to cleanse the house? Send off evil spirits? Or are you looking for something more for your own soul?"

My face freezes, as I have no idea which of those options seems the most appealing to ward off any bad juju in my life right now.

Reid takes my arm gently and walks me a few steps forward. "She just got divorced."

Prudence instantly sighs and begins to grab a few items from the side shelves of the beautiful store. All the items are on display and not cluttered. "We definitely want to burn some rosemary for new beginnings, and sage is a classic choice for around her body."

I smile at Reid in amazement. "Who are you to take me here?"

His grin doesn't fade, and he slants a shoulder up to his ear. "Prudence here gave me a few things when I was going through the big C."

I pause at his admission, appreciating his honesty. No, it's more than that, I admire him at this very moment. Reid was always kind to people, but he had a hard exterior. He feels more humble or vulnerable now, softened a bit.

My thought is broken when I begin to cough from the heavy incense-type smoke appearing around me.

"This will help clear your senses," Prudence explains.

"Yep, clearing my senses is exactly what I need."

Prudence stops and looks at me with a subtle smile, then looks to Reid for a millisecond. "She has a grounded soul, I can sense it."

"Do I?"

"Prudence, go easy on her," he suggests. "Anyway, love what you've done with the place." He gestures to the window.

Prudence smiles, waving a smudge stick in front of me. "Thanks. Always take it up a notch during this time of year, sales pick up." She walks away from me and gathers a few things, herbs, candles, and I watch curiously. "This should all work."

"Oh. Can I pick it up later? I haven't moved yet."

Reid interrupts, "I'll hold onto it for you."

My eyes catch with his own. That would mean I see him again in a few weeks. "Okay." Geez, I need to remind myself not to rely on him or be too quick to answer.

Prudence puts everything in a bag with a dark purple bow. "I threw in some mugwort to help bring out your adventur-ous-in-the-night side." She smirks at me then changes her demeanor to matter-of-fact. "Have you checked out Count of Choc?"

I snort at the name. "As in a reference to Dracula? The cereal? Or like the Count of Numbers from Sesame Street?"

"Exactly, but chocolate. They have a special chocolate right now with hot chilies and cinnamon, plus cranberry chocolate. Only one of those is a double aphrodisiac, though." She smiles confidently at her reference.

"Right." I swallow the odd atmosphere building.

"You two kids have fun. Reid, if you want me to order you some more stuff then let me know, I'm doing an order on Friday," she mentions before returning to where she was making candles.

"Sure. I'll message you," he calls out as he guides me out of the store.

The moment we are back in the sunny afternoon, I make us stand there as I smile to wait for an explanation. "Edible medicine, by chance?"

He clucks his tongue. "It helped when I had cancer. Now I just do it on a very *rare* occasion to celebrate the fact I'm still here. But she meant if I want more herbs to ward off the evil health spirits in my house. Once a season ought to do the trick."

"Okay. I'm on board with that." He looks at me, impressed. "But you're all good now, right? I mean, it's not like you need any extra sage burnings to banish lingering illness spirits or anything, right?"

"Nah. I'm good. Just had a check-up, actually." He flashes me an assuring look. "Besides, I'm your first friend here in Hollows and I would only volunteer if I'm in tip-top shape." He wraps his arm around my shoulders from the side as we continue to walk.

"Lucky me. And you're right that a friend is exactly what I could use right now with my life the way it is," I say simply.

"Exactly." His tone is strong, but when our eyes hold then

it feels like our words are a front for two people who don't feel so confident about our declaration.

It's not that I never thought about dating again. Sean and I separated at the start of the year, but I kind of had it in my head to try and be by myself for a while and find a new routine. Dating the guy who broke my heart when I was young and naïve most certainly wasn't on my radar.

A moment passes, and I breathe out a long puff. "Thanks again."

"Sure. Hey, tomorrow I have this drinks-with-the-dean thing. Want to come?"

My brows knit together. "Sounds... dull."

He chuckles softly as we continue our journey down the sidewalk. "Precisely. I could use the company, plus he has an excellent whiskey collection."

When I think about it, I would only be sitting in my hotel room watching TV and eating pizza. This could be entertaining. "Are you sure I'm not gatecrashing?"

"Nah, he expects everyone to come with a partner, and I could use one event when his wife doesn't try to set me up with their granddaughter." There is a hint of arrogant pride in his tone.

"Ah, there is a hidden agenda."

He stops us and grips both of my shoulders to guide my sight to him. "No hidden agenda. Just nice to take someone who knows me."

"Okay. It's the least I can do since you took me to get my soul cleansed." I try not to laugh. "What are friends for, right?"

The line on Reid's mouth slants halfway up. "Friends."

His tone is faint enough.

5

REID

I pull up to the inn and Lena is waiting for me. She's in a maroon dress that goes to her knees, and she looks like the type of woman that my mother would love for me to bring to dinner. And my cock just let me know he's still alive too.

Lena gives me an astonished look as I park. I quickly get out of my car to circle around and open the door for her. "You drive *this*?" She studies my baby-blue 1967 Ferrari.

"When weather allows," I say and close the door for her after she slides in.

Once I'm back in the car, she gawks at me. "Are we sure you haven't had an early mid-life crisis?"

I laugh as I begin to drive us away. "It's a classic."

I keep the windows open as the top is up, and the wind swirls around us, yet her hair flows just right.

"This is a little too much for the female population to handle. I mean, you driving around town in this." She admires the inside of the car by gliding her hand along the sides.

"Let me guess, you have a mini-van?" I try to focus on the road.

"Actually, just a Prius electric."

A solid choice of ordinary. "What did you do today?"

"Took the train downtown and visited my new office. It's really nice, and everyone seems lovely. My bosses both have kids, so seem quite accommodating. I'll work at home three days a week, which is great. I'm just excited for the projects that I'll be working on, focusing on content," she explains as she looks out the window.

"Sounds promising." I turn right at the stop sign. "My mom says hi, by the way."

Lena angles her body to me and her face floods with extreme interest. "Oh yeah? How is Gwenda?"

"Still your number-one fan and asking why we never dated in college. Don't worry, she subtly hinted that next time she's in town she expects lunch with you." I shake my head in good humor because my mom loved Lena. And as much as I always gave the just-friends speech, my mother didn't quite believe it. She also hated my ex, so I'm well aware she will latch onto the news that Lena has re-entered my life.

"Tell her I say hi, and for sure, lunch to talk about you can go on the agenda." Lena folds her hands one over the other on her lap.

I turn on my speakers that I had installed in this old beast, and the moment the song comes on she glances at me, impressed.

"Pavement, 'Gold Soundz.' Good choice, Professor."

Every time she says professor something inside of me and below twitches. It's far too playful, but not quite flirty.

"My taste in music only gets better with age," I proudly declare.

"I'm sure." She glances at her phone real quick then puts it back in her purse. "Anything I need to know about your colleagues?"

"Nothing shocking. Just be yourself."

She throws me a smirk. "I can do that. Not sure how late this is going to go, but I fly back tomorrow."

"Shouldn't be too late."

We drive along peacefully as I turn onto streets with mansions and well-kept lawns. "I'm just going to warn you, they really are into fall."

"And? It is the greatest season." Arriving at our destination, her eyes re-direct, and she laughs at the scene before us. A scarecrow, pumpkins, gourds, and a witch's broom. "Okay, they have a few decorations," she says, playing down my earlier statement.

I turn the engine off and lazily undo my seatbelt. "Wait until you hear the menu," I warn her with a mischievous look.

I grab the bottle of expensive red wine from the back seat that I brought and come to help her out of the car, although she's already halfway out by the time I reach her. We walk slowly up the long path to the front door, and I watch the sway of Lena's hips on every step, as she's a few paces in front of me, the fabric of her dress clinging to her curves. I notice the way she walks with poise and elegance, and I remind myself that she's doing me a favor.

One of the catering staff lets us in, and after disposing of our coats, we walk to the living room that has people standing and sitting around in various conversation groups.

Immediately Dean Windrawl and his wife come to greet us.

"Reid, so good that you are here." The dean smiles and shakes my hand then turns his attention to Lena, as he is already entranced. "And who is this beautiful woman on your arm?"

His wife is quick to simmer him down by putting a hand on his arm. "Now, Harold, give the young couple a little breathing space. *But* indeed…" She straightens her posture and throws a smile in my direction while fixing her pearl earring. "You've finally come… with company."

Placing a hand on Lena's back, I lead the introductions. "This is Lena Gold. We go way back, studied together out in Boston, and she is moving to Hollows."

"That's wonderful," the dean replies.

Lena smiles politely. "Thank you for having me."

His wife seems to shake off any ideas she had in her head about how to set me up, instead refocusing on her hosting duties. Her hands find her heart. "You two must get a drink, then go to the buffet in the dining room, there are some real treats." She squinches her nose and her shoulders wiggle in delight.

We promise to catch up, then Lena and I head to the adjoining dining room that is decked out with big candles and tables filled with food. There are little cards next to each tray explaining the dishes.

Lena looks around like a kid in a candy store. "Wow, this is some spread." She pulls my arm to grab my attention. "Are you sure it's okay that I'm here?"

"Yeah. This is more a staff catch-up that the dean throws once a semester."

She is quick to smile in relief and immediately begins to study every little label. "My goodness. Butternut squash with smoked cheese, warm brie with walnuts and cranberry sauce, pumpkin hummus…" She walks along, completely engrossed in the scene, then she stops us in our tracks by slamming a hand against my chest. "That's it. I'll become a professor. They have caramel apple crumble. You have the best life," she jokes with me before grabbing a plate for me and then her.

"Oh, thanks. I'm not that hungry."

She gives me a stern-eyed look. "You need to eat, and if you don't then I may just have to contact your mother ahead of schedule. I'm sure I can convince her to get on the first flight out."

I laugh at her banter. "Okay, pass me some cheese, but only because I don't want to hear about my mother anymore tonight." Lena smiles, satisfied. "Want me to get you a drink while you stock up our plates?"

"Team effort, I like that."

I begin to walk away but stop and turn halfway back to her and point a finger. "You didn't tell me what you want to drink."

"It's okay. I'm sure you remember." She says it so easily as she begins to fill my plate.

Two minutes later, I return to find her talking with the wife of Walter, one of my colleagues from my department. I nudge her arm gently and pass her a glass of dry white because she hates red and anything fruity. She offers me an appreciative look as she continues with her conversation about local parks.

I look into my club soda, and Walter comes to my side. "Did you hear about the funding that might be released by the alumni?" he tells me as he drinks from his bourbon.

My sight drags away from Lena to land on my forty-five-year-old colleague. "For one night, you don't want to leave work at the door?"

"What's gotten into you? Normally you are all work and no play. But you're right, except the dean is in a good mood tonight, so it's a prime time to drop some hints for our research project."

I sigh and return my gaze to Lena who is laughing at something. Stepping closer to her, my hand cups her elbow, and she tilts her head in my direction. I lean down close to her ear, and that smell of macadamia nut washes over me again.

"I'll be right back, I promise." My voice is low.

"Of course." She peers up, and if I were to move my feet even an inch then my nose would graze her soft skin, and I nearly groan from the thought.

Departing, I can tell she'll be fine. She was always a social person.

But forty-five minutes later, the guilt sinks in. Finally, I'm able to make an escape from the dean and Walter. The jazz music in the background doesn't distract me from finding Lena in the library off the main hall. I arrive just as Walter's wife leaves. Slowly, I approach Lena whose back is to me as she examines the books on the wall.

She must hear my footsteps, but she doesn't acknowledge it.

I stand behind her and my hands land on her sides, causing her breath to hitch. Our bodies are closer than they should be, but neither one of us breaks the contact. I swear I can feel her shiver.

"My apologies. This wasn't what I meant by accompanying me tonight," I softly tell her with my mouth nearly able to feel her hair.

She turns in my hold and her eyes are genuine and gentle. "Completely okay. Besides, Walter's wife was able to give me a bunch of tips for places to take Oscar and which pediatrician to go to. So *thank you* for bringing me along."

I move to brush a strand of her hair behind her ear. "Any time."

Her cheek moves ever so slightly into my hand, and she inhales my scent.

In another era, I would step until her back hits the books and I would slam my mouth onto hers, and she wouldn't protest.

Our eyes connect, and I wonder if any memories cross her mind in this moment.

I remove my hand and swallow a lump in my throat. "You know, we made an appearance. Do you want to get out of here?"

"Oh?" She seems almost startled by my turn of the scene. "We haven't been here that long."

My mouth quirks out. "It's fine. I've spoken to the dean enough, and hopefully, you were able to get seconds on that apple thing."

She nods and licks her lips. "Okay, if you say so. I have an early flight anyhow."

I attempt to smile in understanding.

———

IT's a quiet drive back to her hotel, and the moment I park my car, the tension could be cut by a knife. I turn the engine off, but I don't move.

"Want me to walk you inside?" I offer. Lena's eyes nearly bug out, which causes a need for me to correct her thoughts. "It's innocent, I swear."

The light from the dashboard only highlights her head tilting to the side in doubt. "It's okay. I think if…"

Thank fuck. I know it would have been a dangerous move.

"If?" I have to ask, as my curiosity is piqued.

She straightens her posture, clears her throat, and definitely looks like a woman who has rehearsed the following words during the drive home. "We aren't twenty-one anymore, I'm not that person. I didn't understand then that you can be intimate with someone and for it not to mean anything. Now I understand. That doesn't mean I'll do it. And we're both smart enough to know that friendship is friendship. I would rather have you in my life than not."

I glide the back of my finger along my bottom lip as I lean against the window. "I get it."

We look at one another for what feels like minutes.

"You'll let me know when you're back?" I hear the fragility in my tone.

Her smile spreads and she leans in to hug me. "For sure. You have my abundance of herbs to ward off bad karma in my home, remember?"

"Right. You need me to help keep those evil spirits away."

She pulls back, with her hand staying put on my shoulder. "Always knew you would eventually be useful," she quips.

I roll my eyes at her humor. "Have a safe flight."

"Thanks."

She reaches for the latch of the door, and I stop her by leaning over to do it for her, causing our bodies to nearly rub against one another until I slowly retreat.

"You smell the same," she says. "I mean, it's spring fresh."

"Don't ruin a good thing, right?" I mention as I sit back.

I slide my hand along her cheek, allowing my thumb to rub her skin. "Thanks again." She may interpret it as tonight, but for me, it's the last few days and an awakening that stirred something inside of me. I was in a rut, with life feeling a little dull.

She doesn't blink, but I notice her eyes glance to my mouth and then directly back up.

"A few weeks," she nearly whispers.

Then she leaves me to wonder why I already feel anticipation for the fact that she's coming back.

LENA

I throw the stuffed lion onto the bed. The finishing touch to Oscar's room. Thank goodness for delivery guys who piece furniture together, because there is no way I would have been able to construct this bed.

A long exhale escapes me as I walk to the doorway. I'm ahead of schedule, which means I have a day to myself since my job doesn't start until next week and Sean won't be here with Oscar until tomorrow. I walk down the hall and into the open-plan kitchen and living area. Grabbing my phone, I lean over the counter to scroll through my contacts.

I know there is someone in Hollows who I could contact. I haven't been avoiding Reid, I simply wanted to focus on the logistics of my move. But my to-do list is now complete.

He's meandered into my thoughts more than I would like to admit. We haven't really texted much since I saw him a few weeks ago—which is fine. Because true friends are the ones who you don't need to communicate with every day, you can just pick up without question. And friends are what we are.

I pull up his contact and quickly type a message and hit send without any big commotion in my head.

Me: Hey! All moved and an official Hollows resident.

I scan the apartment, and I'm impressed with how much I conquered in the last two days. Granted, I barely slept, but I figured I might as well do it all.

The vibration of my phone causes my sight to dart to my phone screen.

Reid: Nice. Need help with anything? I actually learned how to use a hammer and even own a drill set.

Me: Wow. If you have a hard hat, then I may just consider it. But I'm all settled, actually. Could use a coffee, though.

Reid: Coincidentally I'm at Count of Choc, drinking coffee. If you play nice then I may just keep hold of this table.

I smile to myself, as it sounds like a perfect way to end the afternoon.

Me: I can be there in twenty minutes.

He sends back a thumbs-up emoji.

Deep down inside of me, I have an urge to quickly change into something cute and throw on some makeup. But my brain reminds me that it doesn't matter when the guy is just your friend, so leggings and a *We Don't Talk About Bruno* shirt it is.

By the time I get to Count of Choc, my brain is too frazzled over my efforts to find a parking spot to remember that I had nerves buried deep within me.

Reid is sitting at a small table with two coffees in cute little espresso cups, and he is reading a thick academic book. Jeans and a dark t-shirt aren't doing me any favors on the don't-find-him-appealing front.

"Hey, stranger," I greet him.

He smiles as soon as he looks up and slams his book shut. He raises his eyes then looks at me from head to toe.

"Believe it or not, but I totally get your shirt." He brings his arm out to offer me a hug when he stands.

Thankfully we are in a crowded place, which means any tinge of awkward physical connection isn't noticed. Because I haven't forgotten how my body burned from his mere touch when he dropped me off a few weeks ago. Or that for the first time since my divorce, I felt like I was in my own world where I'm Lena and not someone's wife. And if I really am honest, I felt... desired.

"I figured you could go for the hard stuff, so chili-infused espresso just arrived." He slides me a cup.

"Thanks. Exactly what I need." I take a small sip and my tongue instantly stings from the peppery combination. "Wow, I'm now wide awake."

"I would hope so, it's like what, three?" Reid looks at the watch on his wrist.

I set the small cup back on the saucer. "I know, but I've slept maybe five hours in the last two days due to unpacking and decorating."

"Oh yeah, I remember that you are like an organizer extraordinaire."

"That hasn't changed."

He holds his finger up like he has an idea then leans down to collect something by his feet, and he pops back up with the bag from Prudence.

"Think you need this. It's been sitting in my car, so I grabbed it."

I smile brightly, because I love that it's so not Reid nor me, but we are both here for it. "Thanks, I've been counting down the days that I get to do this." There is slight sarcasm in my tone.

"By the way, I'm having a neighbor over later for a drink if you want to come. He's pushing eighty and has some great stories."

I hold up the coffee. "Depends on how caffeinated I am. I would hate to fall asleep on you both. That's cool that you hang with him."

Reid takes a bite of a small piece of chocolate. "Well, he's friendly, plus he had some health issues, so we frequented the hospital together."

I instantly reach out to touch the back of his hand for some sort of comfort. My decision is made. "I'll for sure be there tonight, just send me your address."

He places his other hand on top of mine, and we both seem to look down then up and let go as if our connection may burn our skin.

"You should check out the bookstore in town when Oscar arrives. They'll be having a few readings around Halloween," he mentions. I appreciate his effort to include my son in the conversation, I just never took Reid as a kid person.

"If it's about wizards then we may be in. Actually, I want to find a pumpkin patch or farm then take him to pick out a few."

He leans back against the seat. "Check out Olive Owl. It's an hour from here but worth it."

"Maybe I will." I slide my drink to the side.

Reid brings his hand to weave through his wave of hair. "Oscar's too young, but one of the frat houses puts on a good haunted house for charity."

That does excite me. "Haven't done one of those in years. Sean hated Halloween."

"Was that your first sign it wasn't going to work?" He's blunt, not joking.

I play with my ponytail. "Maybe should have been. But

truthfully, the sign was always there. I thought I was in love, and maybe I was at one point, but in the end, I think it was that I cared. We were right together in so many ways, checked so many boxes, and I thought it made sense because of that. But we were missing excitement as time passed. We both gave clues we wanted an out, and finally, we agreed it was the right step. Sucks all the same."

His brow raises slightly as he takes in my words and understands what I'm saying.

"Anyway, I think I'm too independent to be in a relationship. Maybe I'm not loveable either."

He scoffs at my theory. "You just didn't find someone who can handle your independence. You're allowed to have space in a relationship."

My lips quirk out as I contemplate his thought. I like his theory, it's something that I can believe in. But I don't want to get into relationship talk with the guy who held more cards when it came to me than he knew.

"Can I bring something tonight? I need to stock up at the grocery store anyway. My offspring eats like an entire hockey team."

Reid grins. "Nah, you're good. Just bring yourself."

"Okay. By the way, is this coffee like magic or something? I feel wide awake," I note.

Reid looks at me and leans against his hand, almost smug. "It's because you're in my company."

And I don't think he's wrong.

———

I KNOCK GENTLY on the door of Reid's home. He wasn't exaggerating when he said this place has historic charm. Must be from the thirties, yet the bricks look like they've recently been restored. His apartment is on the ground floor.

Music is playing in the background as Reid opens the door. He's in a dark green sweater that brings out his eyes, and he's happy to see me even though he was expecting me.

"Hey, welcome to casa del Reid."

He holds the door open and invites me in, helping me take my jacket off as I look around. I hand him a bottle of white, just because I don't like to arrive empty-handed. I scan the area and see a lit fireplace, original details on the mantel, and crown molding along the walls. There's artwork on the walls, and a record player stands on a table in the corner, but the music must be coming from a Bluetooth speaker. I feel like this would be a great place to work on papers and relax.

"Want something to drink?" he asks as he heads to a side table with a tray of whiskey in a crystal bottle and matching glasses.

I chuckle softly at this scene. "Wow, you really are feeding into the professor persona."

He pours a glass and then hands it to me. "Would hate to disappoint." I wonder if he meant to have a hint of sexiness in his voice when he said that.

I take the glass since I took a cab here so don't need to drive, and he holds up his own to clink our glasses. The moment I drink the amber-colored liquid, I feel like I'm heading down one dizzy spiral, letting go of something that I can't quite pinpoint.

"Where's your neighbor?" I notice that we're alone.

"Johnny had to cancel, his grandson wanted him at his karate match or something," he informs me so easily and casually.

I try to hide my smile at what feels like a scheme. "So here I am with a fire lit and whiskey in hand."

Reid walks to the sofa. "Not like you had plans."

I follow him and land on the opposite end to ensure there is space between us. "Fair point, and I guess I could use an evening of chillaxing before life gets chaotic."

"I have artichoke chip and crackers. Does that entice you?" he offers.

I rest my head on the back of the sofa. "Wouldn't say no."

Over the next few minutes, I take in more sips of whiskey as the music plays, switching to classic Stars. I focus on the music and allow myself not to think. When Reid returns with snacks, I decide to ask him something that is really none of my business, nor should I care.

"Can I ask you something?" I focus my attention on a cracker, dipping it into the bowl.

"Sure."

"Did you want kids with your ex? I mean, well, you mentioned freezing…"

A subtle smile plays on his lips. "My swimmers? Yeah, I froze some. It's a risk with most cancer treatments that it messes with your ability to reproduce. I can't exactly get someone pregnant now, and kids weren't on my mind even with her. But never say never. That's the thing with life, we evolve, and who you are ten years ago maybe isn't who you are today. Our wants change."

God, everything he says is like he's reading my mind.

"You had a good support network, right?"

He nods yes.

"You? Maryland wasn't exactly near your family."

I set the glass on the coffee table. "I made it work. You make friends, and truthfully, when I had Oscar then it made it easier to connect with people. But even so, I feel like this move is different because it's on my terms."

"That's good to hear, Lena." He kicks his feet up onto the coffee table.

For the next hour, we talk about his travels and the students he's had. There's a list of ones he liked and the others he hated. I tell him about my knitting and the fact that I'm not very good at it. Our conversation flows and time gets lost.

"Another round?" Reid moves to stand up, but I stop him by grabbing his arm to pull him back.

"Not a chance. Age makes my hangover ten times worse, and I would like to be clear-minded tomorrow, and tonight. In fact, I may already book a cab back." But I'm too cozy here.

Somewhere between his story of diving down in the Florida Keys and my desire to visit Santa Fe, I threw off my shoes and made myself comfortable on the couch.

"I would say you can crash in the spare room, but it's my office with a futon that is currently home to boxes of books that I need to donate."

Perfect. A sign from the universe that I should not stay here any longer.

I swing my feet off the sofa, but as I stand, he repeats my own move by taking hold of my arm and pulling me back onto the couch, causing me to land closer to him, in fact, leaning against him.

Our bodies touching is enough for all my senses to grow extra sensitive. I feel the quickening of the blood flowing to my chest.

His smell is intoxicating me; it's not even cologne, it's a simple shampoo that drives most of the female population crazy.

Create space. Yep. Do that.

But he throws his arm on the back of the couch, and I feel like he is subconsciously holding me close.

I peer up at him, and I see that he's looking back at me.

"Is Johnny a myth?" I ask because I wonder if this is all a ploy.

He chuckles and it has a dangerous edge to it. "He isn't, I swear."

"What are we doing?" My voice is breathy, and it nearly sounds like a plea.

Reid's finger gently touches my cheek and then he slides it up into my hair. "Nothing."

"Good. Because I'm smarter now."

The corner of his mouth hitches up due to my comment. "We both are."

"Perfect. Conversations about places to visit and favors of watering plants are our future," I declare.

"Absolutely." He leans in ever so slightly then retreats, as if he's debating.

I bite my bottom lip, close my eyes, and the feeling of whiskey or Reid sends me into a frenzy of floating that I was once addicted to.

Curiosity plagues me, but I don't move.

Instead, he moves closer, and I know what he will do.

But in this chapter of our life, I refuse to make the initiation, because it's still clear in my head the time that I was with Reid, and we played a human game of chess where I never knew which pieces he held.

And this time around, I'm wiser.

This is exactly why I don't give him the chance to let him feel like he is yet again the worthy opponent. It won't be me making the first move.

But I do want a taste, and I'm relieved when his lips gently press down on my own.

I let logic go, and I firmly kiss back, and both of his hands come to cup my face. The tip of his tongue hits the corner of my mouth, and I open my lips to invite him in. A hint of whiskey and a lot of history hits my tastebuds.

The kiss deepens, and my entire body feels lit up, as if a firework is bursting behind my eyelids, and my pussy clenches from a desire reignited.

I murmur into his mouth as he moves to pull my body closer to his own. But as much as I remember this with Reid, it's… different.

So different, I swear it's new.

We part to take in air, only to fuse our mouths together again. Our heads tilt in different angles to get the perfect shape. It turns into a long kiss, a deep kiss, and I grip his arms as if I need to hang on.

I really should pull away.

Instead, I wait for our need to gather air. Softly, and slowly, our lips begin to part, but then he drags his mouth along my jawline and kisses the corner of my mouth.

My chest feels as though it may explode, as my breath is rapid. Closing my eyes, I do my best to collect some composure.

When Reid pulls back, he has an almost cocky, sexy look, and I know he has no regrets.

Nor do I.

I swallow and try to avoid his gaze. "As fun as that was, it probably shouldn't have happened," I admit, yet my tone is entertained.

He sits back, with his eyes darkened in neutrality, completely unreadable. "Right."

This time, it's me who sets the rules, and right now, my priority isn't fulfilling my months of no human contact or starting something new with someone. It's in no way a priority to try and be with the guy who I lusted over when I was younger, and if I'm honest, will think about later too.

Reid abruptly stands and offers me his hand. "Come on, friend, let's order you a taxi."

I place my hand in his warm palm, and he pulls me up. "We will forget about this and go back to coffees?" I ask.

"Yep, and watering plants if asked," he promises.

I slowly nod.

There is a long silence before I search for my phone, but then I pause. A thought comes to me, a sort of wonder or a test or a simple natural need. I'm allowed to try things, I'm independent and free to explore.

"Actually... can I stay?" I ask.

7

LENA

Reid reluctantly comes to lie on his bed on top of the blankets. I lie on my side looking at him as our eyes remain locked, with the glow of the side lamp illuminating our faces.

This was my request. Sleeping next to one another because I don't want to feel alone.

The idea of returning to my house where everything smells new sent a shiver down my spine. Not that I don't like my new house, it's just… confirming that I'm alone and waiting for my next chapter in my life. I know once Oscar arrives that it will feel like home, but tonight, I can be selfish because Oscar is with his father.

"Does this distance follow protocol?" Reid asks, entertained, indicating to the space between us.

I asked him if we could just sleep next to one another, and he didn't hesitate.

"It's perfect," I assure him.

I rest my head against the pillow with my hands tucked under the soft cloud. This should be a horrible idea, but it feels like this may be the way it is supposed to be.

"Good. It's probably better that you're here rather than tipsy in the back of a cab. Not sure why I didn't suggest it." He reaches out to comb strands of hair behind my ears, a feathery touch that I welcome.

"Doesn't matter. We ended up here in the end."

The corner of his mouth pulls. "We did."

"Thank you. I didn't want to sleep alone. I've been doing it for months, but I guess I miss contact with another human," I admit. I close my eyes slowly then open them to look into his eyes again. "Not that I'm going to cuddle or anything, I just wanted to feel someone next to me who isn't the size of a six-year-old," I explain.

Reid sighs. "I can imagine." He quickly glances around his room. "I guess I forgot what it's like too."

My brows knit together as I grin. "Oh please, you haven't had anyone here?" Before he opens his mouth, I slam my finger against his lips to hush him. "Wait, don't tell me."

He grabs hold of my hand to pull me away. "Then I won't. Instead, I'm going to ask you if you want a shirt of mine to sleep in?"

I snort a laugh. "If I undress out of anything then we have no hope of making tonight work." Because we both want to explore this chemistry crackling between us, that I'm certain of.

"Fair point."

We both lie there for a few beats, taking in the moment, sinking into the mattress and feeling the buzz from the alcohol—no, that's a lie, it's from the electricity between us. Attraction was never the problem.

"I have a confession." He looks at me, intrigued, so I continue. "Way back after we graduated and I had a business trip to Atlanta, and I had messaged that maybe we could meet for a drink after my meetings, and you said great. But at the last minute I canceled."

"Right. Like, what, nine years ago? Your meeting ran over or something."

I shake my head gently. "I lied... I didn't trust what seeing you would do to me. I can say that now because I moved on from you. Crazy, isn't it?"

It's insanity maybe because no human has a right to affect someone as much as he did. Over time, I learned that it's what life does to us. It makes us cross paths with people who prepare us for the other people we have yet to meet. Because by the time Sean came around, I thought I knew the signs of what a real relationship that holds promise looked like. I imagined it was stability and everything that was the opposite of Reid.

Reid grazes his fingers along my arm in a soothing motion as he takes in my words. Then he swallows and says, "I see... well, since we are speaking truths then I guess I should tell you that I didn't write to you about my cancer because I didn't want to interfere with your life, your married life. And Tamara hated the idea of me contacting you, she made an ultimatum. But it all worked out the way it was supposed to."

"I guess so." I nod slowly in agreement, but I'm not sure to what. Where we are now or the fact our last chapter of life was supposed to be with other people? I don't dwell too long, because sleepiness hits me, and my eyelids grow heavy. "I'm happy you're here," I say drowsily.

"Because my bedfellow qualities are top-notch? I respect the invisible middle line, my body gives off heat, and my mother picked out the finest sheets on this side of the Mississippi?"

God, I appreciate his effort to lighten the mood, which is

exactly why I smile. "So far, no complaints. Should we try and sleep?"

He nods and quickly unclasps his watch, and he leans back to set it on the bedside table before turning the light off.

We both adjust in the bed but don't dare get under the sheets, and instead, he tosses a throw blanket on us as we lie there fully clothed.

"Permission to move you?" he whispers.

I mumble agreement, and he responds by taking hold of my leg and tossing it over his leg, which brings us closer. I guess we are going to cuddle after all.

"I'm impressed that you haven't tried to persuade me to fall into your wicked ways after that kiss," I remark.

Reid laughs under his breath. "I threw cold water on my face when I went to the bathroom if it's any consolation."

"Thank you."

"Night, Lena."

And then we fall asleep, completely in an unnamed state of connection between two people.

———

WHEN I WAKE the next morning, the bed is empty. Reid warned me that he had an early start, which is why he emerges from the bathroom fully dressed and drying his hair with a towel.

"Morning," he greets me.

I feel like I may blush. "Good morning."

We look at one another with almost giddy looks.

He clears his throat and throws the towel to the side. "I could probably whip up coffee if you want one."

I hold my hand up and swing my legs off the bed. "No,

it's okay. I need to get going, as Oscar arrives later, so I'm going to order a taxi since you have class."

Reid slowly nods, and his lips roll in as if he's stopping himself from talking.

The next few minutes we both busy ourselves with getting ready. When he brings me my jacket, I wonder if we completely just ruined our reconnection in this part of life.

"You won't run away, will you?" he asks, and I could swear there is fear in his voice.

That's comforting because it means he doesn't want to lose our friendship either.

"No, I won't. I promise I'll be in touch."

His expression falters into relief, and he holds up my coat to help it onto my arms, perhaps lingering longer than needed when it slides up my shoulders. Leaning to the side, he opens the front door.

"I'll hold you to it," he warns me, and God, his smirk is… well, it's suave and so damn cocky.

"I know."

He gently touches my shoulder to stop me and then leans in to kiss my forehead, and I feel my body clench from a swirl of desire he just sent through me. I like attentive Reid, it's new but fits him well.

"Enjoy your day," I whisper. He scoffs a sound as if I said something crazy.

Walking away from him, my feet follow the path, with leaves crunching underneath my shoes. The weather has changed in the last few weeks, with trees shaking off the old, so in spring they can welcome the new.

And just like a tree in the changing of seasons, with Reid, I am somewhere in between.

8

REID

Walking along Main Street with Johnny, my neighbor, by my side, I'm listening to him tell me that I look different.

No shit.

I've had Lena on my mind. Her lips are better than I remember, and her doe eyes are now more determined, probably to keep me at a distance. And I get it.

But then we laid next to one another, and comfort never felt so warm.

She has a lot at stake, and I'm just clueless about what the hell spark she lit inside of me when she walked back into my life.

"You didn't need to accompany me, I'm a big boy," Johnny reminds me for the fifth time since I picked him up and brought him to get his eyes checked. "But by all means buy me a coffee since we're out anyway, and none of that pumpkin latte crap." The old man is the most entertaining neighbor I could ask for.

"I know, coffee, strong, with sugar and a dash of cream," I say.

He nudges my arm. "And while we're here, could we get a real magazine, please? The local Hollows press is killing me with the five-page feature on hayrides."

I grin because his grumpiness is the opposite of his personality, as he is the most positive person I know. "Sure, the bookstore is up here."

We continue to walk, taking in the beautiful fall day. "So, do you have another date?" he asks.

"Date?"

"Yes, with whoever is causing you to smile more than I've seen in the last few years. You could power the electrical grid with that smirk that's fixed on your face."

I roll my eyes, but I can't deny that his observation is true. Stopping us, I angle my body to him and slide my hands into my pockets. "No dates. We're just friends."

Johnny waves off my statement. "They all say that."

"Our history and current circumstances really do make us just friends."

"For now," he corrects me. "Have some faith in fate, kid."

I gently shake my head. "Believe it or not, I do. But in this instance, I'm not exactly clear on my thoughts. Plus, I really want to respect the fact that she could use a friend now. She divorced earlier in the year and has a little boy."

"But she also has a history with you, no?"

She does. She really does. And the more I see her, the more it comes back to me, but in a way where I'm watching a movie. I'm not reliving it, only now realizing that it was another time. This time isn't the same, but I haven't figured out why.

"I think we need to find you that magazine, and please tell me it's about history or politics. I don't need to be buying you something that I wouldn't want my sister to know about." I touch his arm and guide him in the direction of the bookstore.

Opening the door, we walk in and it's fairly busy. We head to the magazine shelf, but halfway there a little boy nearly runs Johnny over, causing the book in the child's hand to fall to the ground. I quickly lean down to help pick up the book.

"Oscar, there you are." I already recognize Lena's voice. The voice I haven't heard since a few days ago.

When I look up at the little boy, I see a pair of blue eyes staring at me curiously and a wave of dark hair on his little head. I recognize him from a photo that Lena showed me.

"Oh, hey," she sounds surprised.

Slowly, I stand and hold out the book. "Small world, small town, even smaller bookstore."

My eyes connect with Lena's then bounce back to Oscar.

"Sorry he ran into you, he's a tad excited," she mentions. She pulls him close to her body, and she has a few children's books in her hands.

Johnny clears his throat, clearly eager for an introduction.

"Lena, this is my neighbor Johnny. Johnny this is Lena, my old friend I was telling you about." I can't stop staring at her, my brain witnessing her in all her mom glory. A different kind of glow graces her face today.

"Ah, so you're not fictional. Nice to meet you." She gives Johnny a little wave. "This is my son, Oscar."

Johnny slaps my back. "You didn't tell me she was breathtaking," he mumbles.

Clearly, Lena heard, as her eyes dart to me, and she blushes softly.

I awkwardly smile this situation off and pat Johnny's shoulder. "He's a talker."

Lena looks down at Oscar who is watching his mom with interest. "This is Reid, he's a friend of mine, and we went to school together when I was younger."

The boy looks at me, studies me, then returns his gaze to Lena.

She rubs his shoulder and smiles tightly at me. "Shy at first sometimes."

"Understandable." Remembering that I have a book in my hand, I offer it to Oscar. "Think you dropped this." He reluctantly takes it from me and mumbles thanks. "Looks like you both found something."

"Yeah, we came in because there was a reading hour about magical scarecrows, and I told Oscar that he could pick some books for his new room." She gushes over her son because he is the light of her life, a fact I realized within five minutes of our reunion last month.

"Magical scarecrows? That's… new." I chuckle and scrub a hand across my face because I can't stop looking at them. I swear her eyes sparkle at me, and I seem to have lost my ability to talk.

A fact supported by Johnny who pipes in, "Have you tried the hot chocolate at Ginger & Co.? I know we have Count of Choc, but Ginger's is so much better."

Oscar's eyes light up, and he speaks in hushed tones to his mother. She smiles as if she was expecting his question. "Looks like that's our next stop," she announces.

"Funny, we were just heading there so this one…" Johnny points his thumb at me, "could buy me a coffee."

"What about your mag—"

His hand lands against my chest. "Coffee, I need my coffee."

"Oh, uh, well, we could all sit together," Lena suggests, slightly unsure but still welcoming.

Johnny is already turning my body in the direction of the door. "She's smart too." He winks.

A few minutes later, after Lena paid for the books and we

all walked a few doors down, we arrive at Ginger & Co. Johnny is quick to walk straight to a table that he feels he needs to stake out.

"Let me get these," I offer as we step toward the counter.

"You don't need to do that," Lena protests.

I hold a hand up and indicate to the barista that I'm paying. "Pumpkin spiced latte?"

"Please."

I lean down to be eye to eye with Oscar who stays close to his mom. "Just normal hot chocolate or do you want the marshmallow treasure that floats on top?"

He brings a finger to his mouth to consider. "Is it rainbow marshmallows?"

"That is an excellent question, but I happen to know that this month they use orange marshmallows for Halloween, and I have to say they are my favorite."

"Really?"

"Yep. You even get a little ginger cookie to go with it and a dollop of whipped cream. Can you handle that?" Oscar nods his head profusely. "Cool. I may even join you."

He smiles, and I notice when his smile is wide that he's missing a tooth. I return to standing and pay the barista. When I turn around, Oscar is running to Johnny and Lena is standing with arms crossed, looking at me with a wide smile.

"You drink hot chocolate with all of that stuff in it?" she asks doubtfully.

"It's been a long time but figured I would get in the spirit. Your son is probably going to drink me under the table, though."

We stand there staring at one another with ridiculous smiles, clearly any potential awkwardness between us gone.

"How was your first week of work?"

"Great, and Oscar had a trial day at school. Goes into the

full swing of things next week."

"I'm happy for you, the work and school part." My eyes are glued to hers; I couldn't look away if I tried.

She indicates that we should join Oscar and Johnny, and I follow her. With drinks arriving not long after, I admire how Oscar attacks his drink with manners that I wasn't expecting for a six-year-old as he carefully uses the spoon.

I glance down at my own whipped cream hot chocolate and smile. I'm here often, but I guess I'm never in the moment. I'm drinking coffee and grading assignments. I don't even think I take the time to inhale or appreciate the scent of fresh coffee. Only now do I realize that just sitting without anything to do is a relaxing relief.

"Surely, you are brave enough to conquer that mug," Lena teases me as she brings her own drink to her lips.

"Of course." I push some cream to the side and then take a drink. Admittedly, the sweetness hits me a little too much, and there is no fucking way I can drink all of this. I look across the table and Lena stares at me with a knowing look.

I mouth, *Okay,* because she's right and hot chocolate really isn't my thing, nor am I sure why I felt inclined to impress the kid.

"Excited for Halloween?" Johnny asks Oscar.

Oscar's face lights up. "Yep. I'm going as a pirate. My mom is even making me an outfit."

Lena ruffles his hair with her hand and a smile on her face. "No pressure or anything, but yeah, I'm making his costume."

I look at her, impressed. "Wow, some skills."

"You know we have the best trick-or-treating in our neighborhood. We give out big candy bars," Johnny mentions as he leans back on the chair and drinks his coffee, taking no notice of me.

My brows raise up and I bring my fingers to play with the hairs around my mouth. "Really? I thought we're the neighborhood with the dentist who gives out toothbrushes," I say, doubting him.

Johnny's stern warning glare hits me. "Nope. Big candy bars."

"Mom, can we trick-or-treat there?" Oscar is now excited and bouncing in his seat.

"I mean, I guess. Reid will have to show us the good spots." She mentions it so simply before taking another sip.

I feel my cheeks raise slightly because it's a good idea. I'm guaranteed to see Lena again, and I have no idea why I had the concern that I wouldn't.

"Come on, let me show you where they hide the checkers. Reid and I play a good game. Do you play?" Johnny asks Oscar as he stands and invites Oscar to follow him.

"Yeah, with my dad." Oscar trails behind him with enthusiasm.

This opportunity leaves Lena and me alone, watching them both, content. A silent pause lingers between us, and when I look at her, we have a short stare-off, and we both can't help a gentle smile from erupting.

She plays with the handle of the mug, flicking it with her thumb, returning her gaze to it. "I'm happy we can just hang, that the other night didn't set us back, you know."

Ah, that's the reminder of why I was concerned things would be awkward between us. Because I kissed her senseless and I'm thinking it's a great idea to do it again. Then I let her lie in my bed while I watched her sleep until I fell asleep myself. It was a temporary solution to our needs, because apparently, we both missed having someone around.

"Sure." I keep my internal thoughts down. "He's a great kid, by the way."

She chortles a laugh. "It's the weekend, so he's normally an angel. For the most part, he is a good kid, but weekdays sometimes, with the busy schedule, then I wonder if I spawned demon qualities in him. Adorable, of course, but nonetheless, I question it."

I feel a lazy smile spread on my face. "You suit it. I mean, you look at peace when he's around you."

She looks briefly off to the side and then back to me. "He's a piece of me, the reason I changed my view on so many things. I miss him when he isn't around and appreciate the time when he's with his dad. Selfishly I get a little more me-time now. But he's the best."

I give her a reassuring smile, my subtle way of letting her know that she's doing well with the way the cards have been dealt to her, because nobody wants a divorce, especially if a child is involved.

"It's sweet that you help Johnny. He seems like a fire-cracker." Lena smirks to herself.

I scratch my cheek as I think of the best way to answer. "That he is. I guess I keep my weekends pretty laidback. With my ex, every weekend we had this or that to go do, but for the last year it's been maybe too quiet, you know what I mean?"

"My quiet and your quiet are in different realms. During the divorce, my free moments were times I wallowed in sadness for the situation, and once I got over it then my spare time became logistic planning for the move. It's great to finally feel like I can breathe normally again in a way." She sits up, almost proud.

"We do need you breathing."

Our eyes dance, and I can't seem to grasp this mood between us. Floating on a cloud yet sitting firmly on the earth.

She lets out a puff of air. "I should probably wrangle Oscar in."

I follow her line of sight and see that Oscar is returning to us holding a board game from the corner selection, with Johnny bundling up his coat.

"I have to head home for the grandkids visiting later, but I know Reid is my perfect replacement. Nice meeting you all. See you, neighbor." He tips his head in our direction.

"Nice meeting you." Lena smiles. Oscar waves goodbye before he begins opening the box. Lena looks at her son, not at all surprised. "Really? This is our game option?" Her tone is unimpressed.

I lean into the table to check and chuckle under my breath. "Game of Life."

"Because we need to relive the trauma of adulthood," she says, sarcastic.

"How about I grab us another round of drinks?" I offer.

She tucks a strand of hair behind her ear. "You don't need to do that; I'm sure you have things to do. I can play with him."

I shake my head. "It's really okay. I mean, it's the updated version, so I can sue and have extra insurance options." I gently touch her shoulder to assure her that I'm completely happy to stay.

And it causes her to have the natural radiant smile that is so subtle yet makes the world turn.

God, I'm happy to see it again.

———

"SEE, I KNEW I COULD WIN," Oscar proudly declares as he hits the finish line.

Staring down at my little blue car that is packed with

seven little plastic people, because I hit twins on a spin, and I don't know how the kid got so lucky because he spun the country house, one adopted child, and a wife.

"I demand a rematch one day," I tell him as I toss my pieces back into the box.

"Since I win, do I get a prize?" Oscar bats his lashes at his mom.

Lena drops her mouth open. "You are so bad." She pokes him with her finger. "I know what you're trying to do, but we will order pizza another night."

My mouth quirks out. "Good prize choice."

"Can Reid come too?"

Lena shrugs her shoulders. "I don't see why not."

"Good." He takes the game to return it back to the corner.

I look at Lena, and her jaw flexes side to side. "I see you still charm people, and my little boy is no exception."

I scoff at her mere suggestion and grin. "Kids love me, and most of the time their moms too."

Shit, I'm flirting again.

She catches on right away. "On that note." Her tight smile doesn't fade as she stands and grabs her purse. "I'll see you soon."

"Are we going to text since we're friends?" I gently punch her arm like we're buddies, my grin permanent.

She finds humor in my attempt to remind us. "Exactly."

Our eyes lock for another second, the room feeling smaller. Luckily, Oscar interrupts us, and we all walk out and then have a round of goodbyes.

As they walk off, with leaves blowing around them, I remind myself that I can either test the waters or do everything in my power not to lose a friend.

9

REID

I tie my laces, preparing to go out for my run. It's Sunday, which means it's a lazy day. Grabbing my phone, I don't hesitate to text Lena to see what she's up to, as it's been a week since I saw her.

Me: Want to meet for a coffee or brunch later?

I go to have a sip of water in the kitchen before heading out into the crisp cloudy day. Turning my music on, I begin to run. For the most part, it's a normal run, with my focus on picking up my speed. But twenty minutes in, my phone pings a notification and I glance to my armband to see the screen show a new message from Lena.

Lena: Probably not today. I'm the last person you would want to see. Total mom meltdown.

Immediately, I stop and take my phone out of the case to phone her. After two rings she picks up.

"Hey. What's going on?" I ask and continue to walk, ignoring that my breath is out of sorts from my run, forgot to pause my timer too.

"It doesn't matter. You don't need to hear me in my mom

moment." I can tell her voice is uneven and maybe she was crying.

I bite my bottom lip, but I can't let this go. "I don't care if you're in a mom moment. Come on, let me pick you up in an hour so you can get out of the house. Wallowing in your cute t-shirts isn't going to get you anywhere."

She sighs. "I guess you have a point."

"Good. See you soon."

Screw my run. I turn back to head home, shower, and change.

An hour later, I'm waiting outside of Lena's place, and she approaches my car with a sad smile. Opening the door, she slides in and gives me a peculiar look.

I laugh. "I left the Ferrari in the garage since the weather has turned, so you get my Ford SUV—the key to surviving Illinois winter."

"Wow. It's just…" She looks around the car. "I'm now expecting like a box of twenty jars of mayonnaise or something in the trunk because you did errands and went to the bulk store before going to another store because there was a sale on towels, you know?" she jokes.

I have to laugh at her humor. "Funny."

She shakes off her adjustment to the car and returns to her somber mood.

"You're brave for having me in company today," she says as she buckles up.

"Why?"

She sets her purse on the floor. "It's silly, I guess. Oscar is with his dad and grandparents in Wisconsin, and he was supposed to come back today, but he has the stomach flu and his dad doesn't want to drive with him for two hours. We were supposed to do Thanksgiving tomorrow."

Lines form on my head. "It's only October."

She nods her head and gives me an exasperated look. "I know, but we were going to do Canadian Thanksgiving since he's going to be with Sean's parents for the US version. The joys of divorce scheduling."

"Have you ever been to Canada?"

"Nope. Anyway, I was looking forward to tomorrow since it's a long weekend for Columbus Day, so Monday is off. It's more that I'm disappointed, you know?" She rests her head against the seat and rolls in my direction.

I focus my attention on her. "I can imagine. Do you think your ex did it on purpose?"

She blows off my suggestion. "Nah, I spoke with Oscar on a video call and he looks horrible. I get it, I wouldn't want to be driving if he's throwing up every twenty minutes either. I can't fault Sean for his reasoning. I guess this is a warmup for all the holidays that I won't have Oscar."

I hate seeing her down, and I think quickly of how to change her day. Moving the gear shift to drive, I know exactly where to take us. "I have just the thing to distract you. Do you trust me?" I look to my left for any oncoming traffic.

"I do." A whimsical smile graces her tone, and I like the conviction in her voice.

"Good. Let's hope you feel that way in two hours."

———

LENA RUNS out of the house screaming at the top of her lungs. A man with a chainsaw chases her. He came out of nowhere as we were finishing the haunted house.

I was mentally prepared for that surprise at the end because one of my students had mentioned it. However, I chose not to disclose it to Lena and ruin her fun.

As we end up after the line and the chainsaw man disappears, Lena hunches over with her hands on her thighs to catch her breath.

"What the fuck was that?" She sounds in shock, but I can see she's grinning ear to ear.

I can only laugh as I touch her arm to help her get some stability. "I told you it was a haunted house, and the frat boys took it up a notch this year."

She looks at me as if I'm crazy. "It was a fucking chainsaw!"

"Um, to be fair, they took the chain off for health and safety reasons, *and* you had a good time because of it." I grin proudly at the way I turned her day around.

Lena quirks her mouth side to side. "Okay, you do get a point for that. Oh my gosh, I can't even think what it would be like if we came at night when it's dark, I would die."

"I wouldn't let you die."

"Come on, I owe you an apple cider." She begins to walk toward where they're selling drinks and interlaces our arms.

A few minutes later, we each have a paper cup filled with cider. "Thanks for this. I guess I just needed some fresh air," she mentions as we walk down a path surrounded by trees, as the fraternity house is near a park.

"Any time." I notice she's kicking around a few leaves as we walk. "This is your season; you should be in your element."

She glances up at me with a smirk. "I am. I just had a moment."

"Considering you can now walk with a smile then I'm going to guess that your coping methods have changed since college. You seem a little less uptight, and don't kill me for saying that." Because she used to have a lot of panic attacks, often over little things. Coping with stress wasn't her forte.

"I learned how to breathe." Her words catch me off guard,

and she looks off into the distance in admiration. "It's always a good sign when the version of yourself that you are happiest with is the one in this moment and not the past. I never want college-me back." She scoffs a laugh. "And you?"

I blow out a breath. "Definitely like today's version of me. I'm pretty chill, still turn heads, and I've realized that life is unexpected."

"You, of anyone, can understand that the most."

"I like who you are now. You're even better than before."

She looks at me, puzzled. "Thanks, I think. You're not bad yourself."

"I guess we both lucked out then." We smile in agreement before we continue to walk with our arms grazing. "Were you ever happy in your marriage?" I realize what I just asked. "Sorry, not really my business."

"No, it's okay. I can honestly say that we had great moments, and for that chapter of my life he was the one. But we also had a lack of moments, and it isn't sustainable for the long run." She sounds at peace with her thoughts then loudly exhales. "I think that I developed a theory that you can't have both. You can have the one who will care for you, check the boxes, or the one who will bring you passion and nothing else. You don't get both."

"Huh."

She side-eyes me. "Your ex was both?"

I groan softly and tilt my head to the side. "I guess it was maybe at one time, maybe one-sided, though. I was devasted when she ended the engagement, but after a while I realized it just wasn't meant to be."

Lena touches my arm. "See? Humans maybe aren't meant to get both."

My eyes go wide from that theory. "Wow, we just took a turn to the dark side on this conversation."

It causes her smile to erupt again. "Never in a thousand years would I think we would be talking about this." Her tongue glides along her inner cheek. "Anyway, do you want to maybe go to the grocery store and get a few things so I can cook dinner?"

My face must show that I very much agree with that plan. "Absolutely no objections from me."

We continue on our stroll, walking back in the direction of my car, and we both notice a young couple looking at their baby in the stroller.

"Ah, they have no clue what's in store. They're still in the everything-is-peachy phase, the baby is young," Lena notes.

"You wouldn't do it again?" I wonder.

She looks straight ahead. "Marriage? Maybe. Big wedding? No way. Kids? I honestly don't know." Her tone is clear and confident. "You, Reid?"

"I've never tried any of those things. But I'm not sure. Probably not, but never say never."

"I kind of pictured you ending up with someone ten years younger who probably has a tiny dog and detests kids. Or who was into inviting someone else into bed to make it a party."

I smirk at her suggestion. "Wow, that's some image. And for that, I'll say that you will end up with someone… actually, I don't know. But you will be happy again one day."

Her eyes connect with mine in a way that can only be described as delicate.

And if I had to guess what she was seeing in my eyes, it would be someone who is confused about why I don't see her with anyone else, quite possibly because for a second, I picture her with nobody but me.

———

I STOP Lena from moving any more dishes off the table. Collecting ingredients was hysterical, mostly because we listed all the things you could do with a squash. We ended up listing 103 things by the time we hit the checkout.

Now we're at my place, with a fire on, music soft in the background, and we just finished wild mushroom tortellini and pumpkin pie.

"It honestly is a crime to humanity that pumpkin pie isn't available ready to be bought at the store all year. I don't mean that canned stuff, I want it ready to go at my beck and call." She licks her spoon and then sets it on the plate.

"Clearly you are in better spirits, so I don't need to check in again," I say as I bring a few plates back to the kitchen.

She follows me. "Totally okay. Plus, we still have that bottle of wine in the fridge."

I set the dishes in the sink to wash later, and when I turn around, I see Lena is closing the fridge door with the bottle of white in hand. She studies it. "Olive Owl. Isn't that the place you mentioned?"

"It is." I grab two fresh glasses from the cupboard.

I take the bottle from her to open. The sound of the cork popping is somehow louder than normal, quite possibly because we are alone and something is stirring between us. There's a mix of honesty and tension that keeps the air warm.

Lena leans against the counter as she watches me pour our wine. She tilts her head in different angles, and I realize she is studying the front of the fridge. "It's your cancer-free anniversary?"

I look at what she's studying and hand her a glass, and I see a card from Prudence. "It was the other week."

She looks at me with slight amazement. "It's a big deal. I didn't even text you or bake you something. We should toast to this occasion."

"I don't make a big deal about it. But if we need something to toast about then what the hell." I hold my glass up.

She smiles slyly, as she is amused that I'm so casual about it. "To Reid and his balls." She freezes when she realizes what just slipped off her tongue.

Ah, she's playful.

My grin grows. "That is something to celebrate."

Our glasses clink and then we both drink with our eyes locked.

"I'm sure your package works just as spectacularly as before." Her tongue darts to the corner of her mouth before taking another sip, albeit almost nervously.

I set my glass down. "As much as I love this ego boost, I want to know if you remember what it was like between us." I step closer to her, and I feel a heaviness in the air.

She scoffs at my thought, looks into her glass, then takes another decent sip of wine, but more to occupy herself to avoid the fact that the space is closing in around us. I notice her breath pick up, and my mind is screaming to respect our friendship route.

Alas, I'm cutting myself loose, with every intention to pursue her at this very moment. Everything inside me craves her, and I don't think it will go away.

Lena doesn't move as I step closer and closer. I take the glass from her hands to set it to the side. "Tell me to walk out of this kitchen," I request with an edge in my tone.

"It's your home," she challenges.

"And you're in my kitchen," I counter.

"You really think that I would forget?" she says simply in a quiet tone.

I grab her wrists by encircling my fingers around her. "We've had a lot of life and years since then."

She stares at my hands on her. "You have no idea what problem you created in my life."

"Want to talk about it?"

She gently shakes her head. "Everything inside me is warning me, but my curiosity is too strong."

"I sound like trouble then, because I'm curious too."

An easy smile forms on the corner of her mouth as I close our space, causing her to back against the counter, stuck between me and nowhere to go.

Letting her wrists go, I sweep my hands up to cradle her head, pulling her mouth to me. I lean down to land my lips on hers and slowly and firmly kiss her. It's the kind of kiss that makes me question my intentions because I can't deny my attraction to her, but something else floats inside of me that is undefinable.

But at this moment, all logic leaves me, because I want to consume her and have her writhing under me.

I pull back gently to brush my lips along hers, and I feel her quiver. I look deep into her eyes for a sign to stop, but I only see fuel to continue. I cover her mouth with mine, our tongues dance, and her murmur gets lost in our kiss.

It's the signal for me to continue our evening.

In a quick move, I step back, grip her hips, and spin her around so her back is to my front. God, cinnamon and pumpkin, that's what lingers on my tongue as I inhale the smell of her hair.

I wrap my arm around her to ensure she is flush to my body, feeling what she is doing to me. With my other hand I gently grip Lena's hair to take control of her. I trail my lips along her neck that is on offer as she tilts her head to the side.

"I want to explore every inch of you, the way you are now," I whisper against her hot skin under the shell of her ear.

"You're still a little demanding, I sense." She's taunting me, considering her ass is wiggling against my hard cock.

I chuckle deep in my throat. "And that's exactly what you want." My hand around her waist roams lower, causing her breath to hitch. "I remember the way you used to come on my hand before I would take you deep. You loved getting on all fours for me, showing me your ass."

She gasps a sound, and I feel her melting into my arms. "Fuck," she curses through a thick breath, as she's losing stability.

"You moaned like crazy, and fuck, your face when you would come all over my cock. I can't wait to watch your beautiful face do it again."

It's only a few seconds, but I decide patience isn't for me right now. In one go, I pull down her tights and allow my fingers to feel between her legs.

Soaking satin panties. She's been wearing this all fucking day.

"Put your hands on the counter, Lena, and don't move."

She obeys and doesn't glance over her shoulder as she tries to breathe through her moan. My finger sneaks under the fabric to slide along her slit. Reaching her clit and circling that little bud, her moan grows louder to a near pant.

"I could slide right into you," I warn her as I continue to stroke her. Either my words or movement causes her to gasp in approval.

But I need more of her, so much more. Releasing my fingers from her pussy, I reach both of my hands around to grab onto the line of buttons on her blouse, and without remorse, I rip them open to allow the blouse to fall off her shoulders, and I hear the sound of buttons landing on the kitchen floor.

I graze my lips down her spine, stopping at her bra strap,

my teeth playfully pulling on the band. It's only for a moment, as I unhook it so that the bra too lands on the floor, leaving Lena in just a skirt hanging wildly on her waist. Instantly my hands find a home, cupping her two globes with hard nipples inviting me to squeeze them. I just want to play with her, touch her, make her crazy, fucking mark her. It's pure and simple—I can't get enough of her.

Lust blinds me at this moment; the only sign that I'm on earth is her hand reaching behind to cup my cock.

"You want my cock inside of you?" I murmur against the skin of her cheek.

"Uh-huh, Reid, yes." Her throaty, hoarse breath is my undoing.

Finding my belt, I unbuckle and pull it from the belt loops in one swoosh. Her entire body trembles, and I know just the way I'm going to take her.

LENA

I gasp and quiver at the same time, the sound of Reid's belt coming undone the signal that this is happening.

A thought tries to pop into my head, but I quickly kick it out because all my focus is on enjoying this moment. I already decided that my curiosity deserves to be put to rest.

I lick my lips and reach behind to feel the fabric of his boxer briefs, as his zipper is down. He's hard, long, and ready. I grip him through the cotton, and a gruff sound escapes him. It's quite possible that we have both turned into feral animals—as proven by the fact that his hands yank down my panties with a demanding force and zero patience.

I'm bare and easy for him to do as he pleases, and I already know that I will surrender to whatever he does because the kiss was the key to unlocking a passion I experienced long ago.

He pulls my hair slightly, my neck lengthening and on offer for his mouth. His teeth gently nips at my skin every so often as his lips explore my body. I turn around to face him, and I don't have a chance to search his eyes because Reid flashes me a devilish smirk before he lowers down to his knees and then tips his chin up, his tongue dragging from my knee up my thigh.

"Fuck." My head falls back, and the tickle of his short beard only intensifies the fact that I'm sensitive. My curse doesn't deter him, and he continues his adventure upward, coaxing my thighs apart and splaying me open.

His breath lands on my pussy, and I clench, trying to get more. I need him to do more and fast. The sound escaping my mouth is an impatient moan.

The moment I feel his tongue explore my pussy, I hold onto the counter, trying to keep my balance. Closing my eyes, a warning slips into my mind for a second but then floats out the moment Reid's tongue hits my clit. My body's desire is overtaking any logic, and I tilt against him.

My impatience causes him to chuckle, and after a few more strokes, he's up at my eye level. We both have a dark look in our eyes, unable to blink, completely in a trance.

Except he knows exactly what to do, because Reid's fingertips are roaming up my stomach, teasing me like a feather before landing on my nipple to pinch, our gaze never breaking. He steps closer, his look determined.

"I'm going to take you."

I feel the corner of my lips tug. "I think that's the point."

His cheeks raise, and I know he's trying to suppress his grin, before his mouth covers my own for a damaging kiss, his hand resting on the back of my neck to angle my head against the slant of his kiss. It's his way, as he only does commanding in the bedroom.

Point proven by the fact our bodies press closer, and he's encouraging me to spread wide, all while he places quick kisses down the line of my throat.

I push his boxers down and pump him a few times, then

he moves to take my hand away, raising it up above my head against the upper cabinet.

"Should I…"

I know what he's asking, and I remember what he told me. I shake my head no, he doesn't need to grab a condom, indicating that we are good to go.

The feeling of his tip dragging along my slit and then entering me makes me flinch for a second.

"Fuck, Lena, you are very tight. Soaking wet, but tight," he mentions in a whisper, careful to move slow. "Wrap your legs around me, be a good girl." I follow his request, bringing my legs up around his waist.

I give up on keeping my arm above my head because I need to hold onto something, especially when he pushes deeper. I loop my arms around his neck, my nails digging into his upper back, and I still can't get enough.

He continues to pound into me, I would say ruthlessly, but I think both our bodies are in shock that we're doing this again, and nobody is complaining.

I lean back slightly, offering my breasts to him, and his tongue darts out with the full intention to suck my hard nipple.

"Reid," I breathe, and it's a heavy pant.

"Every time you say my name, I want to fuck you harder." His own breath mirrors my own which causes me to smile drowsily to myself.

I feel like I'm floating. I've completely handed over my body to him, and I'm along for the ride.

We move together, meeting on every thrust until he pauses, his arms looping around my middle and inviting me to hold on.

It's a blur how we make our way down the hall. His pants finally get kicked off when he holds me against the wall to kiss me, as if he needs to remind me that he has every part of me at this moment. And finally, we land on the edge of his bed, Reid hovering over me and inside me, taking me hard and deep.

I use my legs to pull him closer to me, feeling the layer of sweat on our skin. I wrap tighter, but he hums a sound in protest. Instead, his hand comes between us and his fingers play with me. "My way, Lena, and that means you're coming too."

"Better hurry then, because I'm almost there."

A minute later, I begin to shudder around his length, and it must send him off the ledge too. I wouldn't know, as I'm seeing stars.

I'm so wet that I struggle to feel him release inside me, but then I feel his tip twitching, and his face tightens for a few moments before he slowly retreats, holding his weight on one side and breathing an exhale.

When he lands on his back, I can't help but smile as I study him.

He glances at me with a funny look. "Too soon to ask if I get better with age?"

I laugh at his joke and ignore it too. "Is it weird that it was…"

Now Reid adjusts his posture so he can examine me further, his wry smile permanent. "Not bad, I'd say."

"Not bad at all." I think I'm under a spell.

"Guess we can close the book into the curiosity factor."

I have to laugh. "You had that hanging in your head too? The wondering what it would be like to do it again?"

"I am human."

He rolls off the bed, then walks a few steps to turn the duvet back. "Get in, I'll go grab the wine."

"Maybe my clothes too?"

"Not a fucking chance," he calls out as he is already out the door, walking his gorgeous, well-kept naked body through his home. "Don't bother cleaning up either, we're going for round two."

I can't even protest.

I get off the bed and then slide under the blanket, using it to cover myself. At this moment, I take in my surroundings.

My eyes are drawn back to the scene of him walking back into the room with two glasses and a bottle. He wiggles his brows, and his smirk is strong as he approaches the bed.

A minute later, we are both settled in bed with wine in hand.

"So, this day took a turn," I say, but my smile doesn't seem to fade.

Reid holds his wine out to me to clink our glasses. "A perfect way to spend a Sunday."

I nearly choke on my wine. "In your world. In my world this is not a normal occurrence."

He looks at me peculiarly then tries to hide his smirk. "I take it that I'm the first guy you've been with since... well. I took you the way you should always be taken."

My mouth gapes open and I nudge his arm. "I am not talking about this with your mark still inside of me."

Reid lies on his side, holding his drink and staring at me. "Solid observations."

I look away and try to avoid his stare. "But fine. Congratulations, you helped me over the bridge."

He takes my glass and sets our drinks down on the bedside table then plants his hand on my arm. "I'm happy to have done the honors."

I playfully punch his arm, but he is quick to grab my wrist, both of them actually, before he pins me down to the pillow.

He peers down to my mouth then back to my eyes. "You're beautiful." His tone is soft.

I try to look away, as his statement for some reason surprises me. He is quick to crook a finger under my chin to guide my gaze back to his. "Don't look away."

"Geez, you really are still kind of demanding," I quip.

"And you are spending the night."

My brows raise. "Because you said so?"

"There are a few more things that I need to do to you. There was never anything you didn't want to try."

Bedroom Reid is kind of cocky, which makes him sexier and causes our attraction to be untamable too.

"Well." I blow out a breath. "It is a long weekend, so I guess logic can go out the window for a night." I hear the hesitation in my voice, the warning inside my head, and feel that other muscle working in my chest even though I swore to myself it needs a hiatus.

Reid taps his finger to my lips, his look pure accomplishment.

He rolls back and holds his arm out, inviting me to lie against him. Cuddling was never really our thing, I mean, we did it occasionally, but Reid was more a to-the-point kind of guy. Reaping the benefits and back to his busy calendar when he was done. It was our arrangement, and even though I knew I wanted more, I never told him, only hoped. This? I'm not used to the kiss on the top of my head that he just gave me.

But my body is already a traitor, and I nuzzle into him closer, inhaling the scent of his cooled-sweat skin and my fingers tangling into the short hairs on his chest.

We lie there in a long silence, but peaceful and right.

"Why do you think the universe made us end up in the same place?" he asks simply.

"I don't know, but when I figure it out then maybe I will

tell you, as long as you promise me coffee and pie," I nearly mumble as I get cozy in this position. I draw lines along his torso with my finger, and I pause when I feel his small scar.

"Noticing something new?" he remarks in a drowsy tone.

I touch the small line just above the area that is recovering from fucking me with what felt like purpose.

"It was a small surgery to remove some of the tumor near my testicle before I started treatment. Amazing what they can do with a keyhole procedure, and I was home two days later." He explains it with a blank tone.

I peer up at him as I rest my chin on his stomach. "You're here."

"Let it go. I haven't lost any talents, so we have no reason to wallow."

I snort at his answer, and yet again feel astonishment for his strength.

He wraps his arms around me and slides me up his body until our mouths are at the same level and I'm fully on top of him. "You know something that hasn't changed in all these years?"

"What?"

"I still like you better when you're naked."

I roll my eyes. "Go to sleep, Reid."

He kisses the top of my head again before he strokes my hair. I sense his breath growing deeper, which in turn causes me to follow into a lazy slumber.

It's been months since my divorce was finalized, which means months since I laid with a man after sex.

But it's been years since I've felt a fire inside of me when a man kissed me. That realization is the risk that I knew I was taking when I decided to invite Reid back into my life by sending him a message.

The risk that is now a fact.

11

LENA

Of all the positions we could choose to complicate matters, we find ourselves like this. Me straddling Reid as he sits in the middle of the bed, our arms entangled and bodies tight together. Our mouths fused and his tongue flicking my own. A long kiss, before our mouths slowly part, and our eyes are locked as he holds my hips and I move.

We have no haste, we just simmer in this position with the sun peeking through the curtains.

He kisses my shoulder, before whispering in my ear, "I like the way you look when you come."

That only makes my walls squeeze his cock and want him deeper. "And I like it when you come inside me," I reply before I nip at his neck, dragging my pussy up to his tip before plunging back down on him.

"Just like that," he encourages me.

I repeat my movements, wanting to bring him to his downfall.

I kiss him to avoid looking into his eyes, but his hands

come to hold my head in place. "Look at me." He has a sort of urgency in his tone, one I don't quite understand.

When I struggle to obey, he is quick to flip us so I'm on my back and underneath him. Now he is in control, and he taunts me by slowing down our rhythm on purpose, circling his tip inside of me before going in deeper to hit new depths. I moan from his move, and when I reach down between my legs to touch myself, he grabs my wrist to stop me.

He tsks me. "Only I will make you come right now."

Heaven help me. This man is determined in the bedroom.

"Spank me for being impatient, but I'll make it up to you in the shower with my mouth," I tell him, and I love how I'm so… free and not afraid to be this way with him. Because I wasn't this way with my ex-husband, not for his lack of effort, I just couldn't unlock it.

Reid chuckles under his breath, and his head falls into the crook of my neck. "Are you trying to kill me this morning?"

"Oh no, sir, I'm trying to get your heart rate up before breakfast." I throw in a theatrical tone before a smile erupts on my lips.

Reid growls, right before he throws my legs over his shoulders and picks up his pace.

All through the night we've been at this, and I think each time it gets better because we treat one another's bodies as a new discovery, not a path once crossed.

By the time we're both coming, I think I'm completely spent and will have no way of walking normally any time soon.

He collapses on top of me, and I keep him there with my ankles linked together, at home on his lower back.

I stroke his hair, kiss his cheek, and Reid rests his ear against my chest.

"Mmm," I hum. "This is not what we are supposed to be doing," I note. My voice is thick with drowsiness.

"Nah, we're good."

I can't debate him right now, as we're both completely relaxed lying like this.

"I'm going to head back soon. I should get ahead on laundry, and if Oscar is feeling better then Sean will bring him back tonight." I lean over to grab my phone to see if I have any new messages.

Sean: Still has low fever. Ate half a piece of toast, so that's a start. I'll let you know in the afternoon what we'll do. Is that okay?

I'm quick to respond.

Me: Sounds like a plan. Can I call him?

It doesn't take long for a video call to pop up.

"Shit," I curse aloud. Reid looks at me, puzzled. When I show him my phone screen, he gets it instantly. He rolls out of bed and tosses me a shirt. I throw it on, and by chance, it's a college shirt from where we both went, so it won't look suspicious. Reid indicates he's going to head to the kitchen, probably to give me privacy. I scan the room for the best place that looks the least questionable. I nearly spring out of bed and head to the window where I answer just in the nick of time.

"Hey, sweetie," I say as I fix my shirt. Oscar still looks a little worse for wear.

"Mom, I don't feel good." He seems to be lying on the sofa.

"I know, but you'll be better soon." I hate that he's feeling this way. "Did Daddy give you some of the bubble-gum-flavored medicine?" I can hear Sean call out a yes in the background as Oscar nods. "Just take it easy."

"We're watching a pirate movie."

"Again?" I have to smile.

"Yep. Where are you?"

Crap. I stall for a second then throw out a lie. "Just went to get a coffee in town."

"Oh."

"Go get some rest, kiddo, we'll talk soon. I love you."

"I know." I give him a look that I'm expecting something more. He sighs. "I love you too."

"So heartfelt," I retort then blow him a kiss and end the call.

After freshening up a little, I follow the smell of food to the kitchen. Standing at the door of the kitchen, I watch Reid crack an egg into the pan. I wish he would throw on a shirt and a sweater, preferably a turtleneck at this point.

He glances up for a second before returning to his task. "All good with Oscar?"

"Yeah," I say as I slowly make my way to the counter to lean over. "Perhaps on the mend soon. Thanks for giving me some privacy."

"Don't sweat it. I understand."

Does he? Because it never even crossed my mind to bring someone else into Oscar's and my life, not in the way that's beyond the friend zone. It's too soon. Oscar needs to settle into a new routine, and I'm not sure what I'm doing with Reid anyway.

More importantly, I won't let my thoughts take over my heart and make me believe that there is a chance for anything else.

Clearing my throat, I observe his cooking skills. "Breakfast is new. Then again, that wasn't really our thing."

His upper lip twitches and then his jaw goes tight to one side. "Want to finally talk about it? We've kind of let that elephant in the room sit on the sidelines the last few weeks," he mentions as he pours me a cup of coffee then offers it to me while I debate what to say.

Taking the mug, I know he's right. "There's nothing to say, is there? I wasn't the one for you, and because of that, I ended up on a path that led me to Sean and ultimately Oscar. It all worked out." I bounce my shoulders and inhale the smell of his expensive coffee, Italian, I think.

Reid leans against the counter with a spatula in his hand. "If you're confident with that theory, then sure."

"I am," I persist and focus on my coffee.

I think I'm in the clear as he works the spatula under the egg. But then, so casually as he flips the egg, he asks, "Why was I a problem for you?"

"What do you mean?" I play oblivious.

"Last night, you said I have no idea what problem I caused."

Shit. It slipped out.

I cluck my tongue inside my mouth. "It's nothing. I'd rather not talk about it and instead enjoy breakfast."

He studies me for a few seconds. "Okay."

I already know it will come back to bite me in the ass.

Reid holds the spatula to the side, pausing mid-thought. "You know it's not because I didn't care for you, right?"

That's what hurt the most, when I realized we weren't ever going to be anything more back then. I know he cared. He cared a lot. When I was having a bad day or sick or simply needed a friend, he cared far too much that it never made sense to me. "I do."

Our eyes meet and linger until the toaster pops up four pieces of toast. Breaking our locked gaze, he reaches over to toss the bread on a plate.

"I forgot to ask, do you take your coffee with milk or sugar? I've only seen you drink pumpkin lattes or chocolate espressos, so that doesn't help me much when I'm serving you the strong stuff." He grabs the pan to divide the eggs between two plates.

"I'm okay today with just black coffee. I think I may need the extra-strong kick." I smirk to myself.

Reid hands me a plate and then indicates to head to the living room. We make our way to the sofa for a casual breakfast. "It's been a long freaking time since I've done the awkward breakfast the morning after," he admits.

"Yeah, I guess your fan club prefers being your sexual entertainment then leaving before daylight," I tease.

"Something like that," he replies, not elaborating.

"But this isn't awkward, is it?" I ask as I play with the fork near my lips.

He smiles softly. "No, it isn't. Actually, far from."

"Good. Because I would kind of hate it if we ignored each other just because we decided our hands all over one another is a good idea."

"An excellent idea, even." His eyes stay planted on me, and I wonder what he's thinking.

"I mean, that adjective may be a step too far, but sure, in the spirit of things. Excellent." Because what we are doing would have my younger self frustrated.

Reid chuckles before biting into a piece of toast. "I should be grading assignments today, but I feel like I need to prove a point with you, plus we still haven't had that shower."

I set my plate onto the coffee table and my jaw goes slack. "You really want to do it on every surface here?"

He shrugs a shoulder. "Why wouldn't I?"

"Don't you have memories here with your ex?"

"Nope. Moved here after the split. Why, would it matter?"

I tilt my head to the side. "Huh, I guess there is still so

much to catch up on. I feel like I should have known that fact, just like your cancer-free anniversary."

Reid takes hold of my hands. "By all means, we can catch up more, but want to take advantage of your day off sans Oscar? You don't even need to get dressed."

Looking down at the fact that I'm in his shirt, I wonder if it's strange for him to see me this way. I ruefully shake my head at his comment and then point a finger at him. "You have papers to grade."

He moves slowly onto his hands and knees, crawling to me across the sofa, approaching me seductively. "I'd rather assess you on all fours while I take you from behind." His mouth lands on the bottom edge of the shirt and his teeth take hold to drag the fabric up slightly.

"You know, considering this all started because we were celebrating your rejuvenated dick, he really is taking center stage on everything that is transpiring," I tell him as my entire body curves up against him.

A deep snicker sounds from the back of his throat. "Nothing's transpiring. We're just having the reunion we were meant for."

I have no clue what his words mean, and because he possesses me then all caution is thrown to the wind, especially when he nuzzles his mouth between my breasts.

———

REID TURNS the engine off as he parks in front of my place. The whole car ride was silent. Because how do you end a night and day filled with laughter, sex, and a connection I never quite understood?

Slowly I unbuckle my seatbelt. "Thanks for driving me home."

"No problem. Stranded and tied to my bed will have to wait for another time," he attempts to joke, and I can see he's kind of nervous, as his finger taps the wheel.

"Another time," I sigh. With confidence, I look at him with a wry smile. "Probably let's not overthink what this was."

Safe option. That's the smart thing to do.

Now Reid has to grin. "Good. I guess I will see you soon for coffee, randomly in my lecture, or when you feel inclined to video call in only a towel—just throwing out some options."

I chortle at him before I escape the car because he makes me feel reassured that we will be alright, and that means my heart may just stay intact.

12

REID

———

Shaking my head, I don't know if I should be entertained or fiercely annoyed. My mother bats her lashes at me before looking at the menu on the wall of Ginger & Co. It was my lucky day when I walked out of my lecture to find my mother waiting on a bench, having just arrived for a surprise visit.

"Don't look at me like that," she chides as she plays with her long colorful earring that matches her knee-length tunic and tights. She's proud of herself for throwing me off course.

But in truth, I'm never not happy to see her. My parents have given me a good life, have hearts of gold, and will never be shy about saying what's on their mind.

"Your father has business in Seattle, and I figured this was a perfect time not to be home alone," she adds.

"So, you hopped on a plane from Charlotte to Chicago?" I sound skeptical of her spur-of-the-moment plan.

I order our coffees, and we head to a table by the window. Sitting down, my mother can't stop smiling at me. She reaches over the table to squeeze my hand before she pats my cheek like I'm seven. "You had such a great milestone the other week. I wanted to take you out to dinner or just… see my boy."

I shoo away her hand and roll my shoulders back. "Here I am."

"Did you do anything to celebrate?"

Without thinking, I say, "I did. I wasn't alone if that's what you're worried about." Shit, I realize the error of my ways when I see her interest is piqued. "Just a good bottle of wine." And hours and hours of orgasms, but I leave that detail out.

She doesn't press. "You look good. This facial hair thing, I was skeptical, but it's just short enough. You seem to be in tip-top shape too." She continues to gush my praises.

I'm thankful when the barista brings our drinks, as it means I may actually get a moment of quiet from my mother; nonetheless, a grin tugs on my lips.

"Would you tell me if I looked like shit?" I wonder.

She waves off my thought. "No, but I swear I'm not lying when I say that you look almost radiant."

I hum a sound as I take a sip of coffee. I should really ask the owners of this place about investment options, I'm here often enough.

"I can't complain about life lately," I tell her, and I feel the smile not fading on my lips.

My mother's eyes blaze with curiosity. "Is there a woman, Reid?"

"No," I point-blank answer.

She sighs then drinks her latte. "I was hoping you would say you finally saw sense with Lena."

"What does that mean?" I scoff, offended.

My mother gives me the do-I-really-need-to-explain look. "I'm not an idiot, I know in college you two were at it like rabbits. Remember when you and your roommate had brunch for us parents and you invited her over? I saw it as clear as day. I liked her, but I know you both went your separate ways."

"She wasn't the one for me." That I'm honest about.

"Then or now?" She raises a brow at me while her lips purse out and she drums her nails on the table.

How my mother knows what to ask is her goddamn talent. Because her question is the one thought that has been lingering inside of me.

Why does now feel different? What I felt back then doesn't feel relevant now. Then, I wanted a career, to be free and not tied down, and I didn't think I loved her. Now, I want none of that, and Lena has changed into a spectacular creature who won't get out of my damn mind.

I get lost in my thoughts for a few seconds and stare at the glass canister of sugar. But my daze is quickly broken when my mom begins to tap the window and move like a jumping bean in her seat.

My eyes dart to what or whose attention she is trying to get. Then dread or pure delight hits me when I realize that Lena is walking toward the door.

There is no fucking way, even if Prudence cast a spell or Hollows worked its weird fall-magic crap, that the chance of Lena being here at the same time is a coincidence.

Glaring at my mother, who tries to hide her joy in the turn of events by keeping the cup at her lips, I know she is up to her tricks.

"What did you do?" I mutter as I wave to Lena who indicates she's going to order a coffee.

My mother bounces her shoulders up toward her ears, and when she sets her mug down, she breaks. "Okay, okay. When you ran into your home to drop off your laptop, your phone rang in the car, and I noticed the name, so…"

"Let me guess, you answered?"

"I mean, Lena has a working-from-home day and needs a coffee too." My mother looks at her nails.

I don't even get to answer, as my mother greets Lena with a bright smile as she arrives at our table.

"Hi. Good to see you again." Lena beams at my mother then turns her gaze to me, and it's reassuring, welcoming, and recognition that I slid into her at 7am a week ago. "What a coincidence that we're both here." Her eyes flash at me, and I hear the sarcasm in her tone, which only causes me to smirk to myself.

"Please, sit with us," I play along.

With enthusiasm, my mother makes space and pulls up a chair for Lena.

"This is so wonderful that you moved to Hollows. When Reid told me, I nearly fell off my chair. It's always nice to catch up with old friends," my mother begins, and I'm waiting for the big reveal of her scheme to come out. "And a mother now too, let me see a photo."

Time swallows me whole as the next few minutes, Lena is showing photos of Oscar, and my mom coos and gives me winks. I can only roll my eyes and pray for a comet to fall on us. Instead, I indicate to the barista for more coffee.

"He is a darling. You make beautiful babies. I can see he must keep your hands full. It'll be hard when his father goes to live in another country," my mother mentions.

Lena wobbles her head from side to side. "It'll be okay, it's temporary. I have a good relationship with Sean's parents, and it was the reason I also agreed to look for a job in the Midwest, because then when Sean returns, he will likely stay in Chicago. But yeah, it's… a change."

"You can rope my son into helping you when needed. I've

seen him with kids, his niece, a natural talent really. Hopefully, Reid will make me a grandma again."

I scratch the back of my neck. "New topic," I suggest.

My mother ignores me and waves a finger between Lena and me. "Your renewed friendship with one another couldn't have come at a better time." My mother turns her attention to me. "Lena makes beautiful kids, so if you ever need a friend to carry your frozen sperm for nine months, then she is a great candidate." She mentions it so casually, not malicious.

Lena sputters out her drink, clearly surprised by the turn of this conversation.

"Holy shit. Is this why you set this up?" My jaw drops and my eyes go wide. I can't believe my mother just said it, but that's my mother.

"Wow, um, I'm… flattered you seem to think I'm a good candidate." Lena doubts her response as she pats a napkin around her mouth.

I shake my head and rub my temples with my fingers. "Ignore my mother. She has zero filters."

"I mean, do it the medical way or add in a little extra benefit to the procedure, your choice really," my mother adds.

Lena tries to hide the laughter that I know wants to erupt.

I turn my attention to her. "Are you sure you're working-from-home day without real coffee isn't looking like the better option right now?"

"Nah, this is kind of entertaining." Lena chuckles and leans back against her chair.

My mother places a hand on Lena's shoulder affectionately. "I'm sorry, that was perhaps a step too far. I'm just very happy that Reid is still here, and there are so many possibilities, you know?"

Lena touches my mother's hand on her. "I can understand."

This instant bond that these two have is something that I never experienced with any exes. It's concerning and makes me uneasy; I'm outnumbered.

"I'm taking Reid out for a big dinner tonight, bells and whistles. Nothing like a five-course dinner with your favorite parent. You should come with us, won't you?"

"Kind of you to offer, but I'm going to pick up Oscar soon from school and then work a little after he goes to bed," Lena politely replies.

It only makes my mother look more fondly at Lena.

But Lena doesn't notice because our eyes meet and speak in their own language, a sort of confirmation that we are both holding on for the wild ride, and I don't mean my mother.

A silence overtakes the table, and my mother must notice, but it's Lena who breaks the quiet. "I should probably head out. The traffic of moms in the pickup line is brutal." Lena begins to move, and she grabs her purse.

"I'll walk you to your car," I offer. "I'll be right back." I give my mother a warning glare not to follow.

She and Lena and say their goodbyes, and when we're outside, I open my mouth, but Lena beats me to the punch.

"So, I'm turkey-baster material?" She tries to keep her laugh down, but she can't.

I can only laugh, relieved that she's taking it all in good stride. "We can't erase this moment, can we?"

She shakes her head. "We don't get to erase any moment, it's now a memory imprinted in my brain. Besides, I really want to laugh about this a year from now. I'm honored, really."

We walk next to one another, and I see her car a few spaces up. "Thanks for making her dream come true. Stopping by, I mean. She showed up out of the blue to surprise me, and this day keeps taking turns."

Lena hits the button on her car key then leans against the vehicle to look at me with arms folded. "I always liked her."

"*Well*, we know her opinions of you." I slide my hands into my back pockets and study Lena for a second. "By the way, you called earlier? Before getting roped into my mother's schemes. Everything okay?"

Lena looks stuck in thought as her mouth makes an O shape. "Right. That." She tucks a few strands of hair behind her ear. "I was just… checking if you were free… for lunch." She tries to avoid my eyes on her.

Something about her demeanor makes me narrow my eyes in amusement. Then it dawns on me what it could have been. "Were you… bored?"

Her eyes snap back into my direction. "No," she scoffs in defense.

"Really?" I'm doubtful of her answer. "Had a break in your video conference schedule and thought we could…" I flash my eyes at her.

She shakes her head and keeps her lips tight, but I see her grin trying to escape. Then she breathes an audible breath and changes the subject. "Anyway, uhm, I was wondering… Halloween is coming up and trick-or-treating. I might need some company, as Oscar is planning a big haul—"

I cut her off. "I'm there."

A shy smile plays on her lips. "Cool." We look at one another, almost giddy for a few beats. Then she surprises me. "Are you picturing it in your head?" Her raised brows and sly expression cause me to know exactly what she is referencing.

I step closer to her, unable to control myself. I plant my hand onto her side, and she inhales a long breath.

"If it's any consolation, I'm sure if I ever wanted to go down that route that it would be the hottest minute of impregnation of your life," I tease her or warn her, I'm not even sure anymore.

She chortles a laugh and lets her head fall against my shoulder, causing me to kiss the top of her head because it just feels natural. I love it, actually; it may be my new favorite thing after being buried deep inside of her.

"You are something," she rasps.

I cup my hand under her ass and spank her playfully, and I search the area to see if anyone notices. "You should get out of here before we get a traffic ticket."

"For what?" Her head perks back and she looks at me, puzzled.

I swipe my hands through my hair. "So many possibilities for public indecency."

She slaps my arm. "I'm leaving." She walks out of my hold with a grin fixed on her face.

I watch her circle around her car and slide onto the driver's seat. She leans her head to look at me through the window. Her lips quirk side to side and she ruefully shakes her head.

When she begins to drive away, I realize that flirting wasn't part of the pact, but she didn't stop me either.

Remembering that my mother is waiting for me and probably trying her best to spy through the window, I sigh and return to the café.

Inside, I approach our table as if I'm hunting, and my mother knows she's in the hot seat.

"Lena is absolutely beautiful. Hasn't even aged and seems like the kind of woman that you need in your life, as a friend or more than friends."

Holding my hand up, I stop her from continuing. "Yeah. Think you established that when you suggested she be my surrogate for a baby I don't even want."

"No. I'm only highlighting a life that maybe you do want. I'm not trying to pressure you."

"Could have fooled me." I sigh as I lean against my propped elbow.

"Really, I'm not. If you want to be single, married, married with no kids, gay, I don't care. But I also know that in the last few weeks when I've spoken with you on the phone, you have a light in your tone that people take notice of. For the first time, I've wondered what has you in a mood that makes me go to sleep in peace at night. And I think it's because there is something lingering inside of you. That woman is stirring things within your soul."

I play along. "Such as?"

"A glimmer of a possibility, making you want things you never wanted before, and I don't mean kids." Her stern look informs me she means I need to pay close attention to the woman that just walked out of here.

I don't try to counter, because you never do that with my mom when she is so positive that her theory is right.

And I can't debate her because she's only saying what I've been thinking myself, and it causes me to smile every night before I go to bed.

"I have twenty-four more hours with you?" I pretend to be inconvenienced.

She smiles, entertained. "I won't say more, because I think she already weighs heavily on your mind."

That she does. I just don't know what to do about it.

13

LENA

Grabbing the plastic pumpkin basket, I search my kitchen counter for any other items we may need.

"Reid is still coming?" Annie asks as she perches on a stool at the kitchen counter. She was in Chicago for a conference so changed her flight to tomorrow to come out to the suburbs and stay with me and Oscar for one night.

I don't look up as I pour a bag of mini candy bars into a bowl. "I think so. I mean, I mentioned you're here unexpectedly, yet welcome, and he didn't sound like it scared him away."

"Why would I scare him away?"

I give her a pointed look. "You have always been... opinionated."

"And? You two are just friends, so it doesn't matter my opinion of him," she counters, and I know this is some sort of psychological trick that she's playing on me, as she is up to date on the latest in my life.

Puffing out a breath, I collapse onto the stool next to her. "I'm a fool," I state. "I'm probably the biggest mixed message out there. I tell us not to overthink it, but I can't stop flirting. I know it's wrong, I know I need to keep my guard up, but Reid, he just does something to me."

Annie grabs a piece of candy and begins to peel off the wrapper. "You are allowed to have fun. You are allowed to have guy friends. And you are allowed to one day fall in love again. You're smart where Oscar is involved, and you don't need to worry about landing on two feet and starting your own life as a single person because you've always been independent, and you have this. You could even have him. There is no timeline you need to follow. In fact, you have a lot of checkmarks happening right now, so why the gloom?"

That ache between my ribs is back, a bundle of nerves that has no idea in which direction to head—my heart, my pussy, my brain, or everywhere.

I grab my scarf that was on the counter and begin to wrap it around my neck. "You're right, except I don't know what the hell I'm doing. Reid, he's..." Before I can finish my sentence, the doorbell rings. "Here." I'm saved from any talk of emotions.

Annie smiles right before I slide off the stool and head to the front door. Opening it, I see Reid's back. He must be watching the kids already walking along the sidewalks trick-or-treating. He turns slowly, and a suave smile forms on his mouth to greet me.

"Trick or treat?" he asks in a sing-song tone.

"What are you?" I ask, playing along, in doubt.

He steps in, causing our bodies to brush together. "The hot professor, of course. Just so happens I wear the costume every day." He holds up a bottle. "Here, for later."

I roll my eyes at his joke as he hands me the wine that he brought.

He leans in, but I'm not sure if it's to kiss me on the

mouth, or maybe I get nervous. I move, he moves, then he kisses me on the cheek, and in a way, it calms me.

Reid walks into my home like he owns the place and heads straight to the kitchen where Annie smiles and says hello.

"Long time!" She stands to give him a hug, which surprises me, as she is not a hugger. Then I see that she's feeling his arms as she flashes me a look of approval.

After a round of pleasantries, all our attention turns to Oscar who comes running into the room. He has a scarf I tied around his head like a pirate, and he's dangling the store-bought eye patch. But the vest and pants are all me and my sewing machine.

"Is it time yet?" Oscar asks as he grabs his basket and pirate map, since fake knives were a no-no at school.

"Look at you!" Reid compliments and offers his hand so Oscar can high-five, to which he jumps up and does. Reid pulls a giant candy bar out from his coat pocket and tosses it to Oscar. "From Johnny since we're staying in your neighbor-hood tonight."

"Wow!" Oscar is impressed with the king-sized treat.

"Definitely getting a photo of you, kiddo." Annie begins a mini photo session on her phone.

I clap my hands together, knowing we need to get moving. "Who's ready for trick-or-treating?"

"Me!" Oscar jumps up.

Annie waves her hand. "If there are hot single dads then I'm so in," she mutters.

Reid looks at her. "That's your thing?"

Annie nods proudly.

I grab my witch's hat and both Annie and Reid look at me, impressed. "Only for a little bit," I justify.

"Is there… more costume somewhere?" Reid subtly asks

as he rubs his stubbled chin. Annie picks up on the undertone and smiles tightly as she walks with her arm around Oscar.

It was all in good fun, but I feel that heat now spreading around the group of nerves that are screaming at me to figure out where to go.

Ignoring it, I meet Reid's eyes and feel like a strand of glue is pulling us together.

———

"Jesus, it's cold." Annie shivers as she keeps her arms folded around her body. We're standing at the bottom of the path, while Reid is up at the door with Oscar to collect candy.

We are about ten houses in. After the first three houses where I accompanied Oscar on every doorbell push and took photos, well, the novelty wore off. Annie and I are instead freezing as we watch.

"One more house, then we can go home. I left the bowl of candy out, but it might need to be replenished," I say.

Annie tips her head in Oscar's direction. "Reid is good with him."

"I guess." I keep my answer simple. But yes, he is, and that should be my reminder. Friend Reid means there is no chance for Oscar to get hurt.

"*And* I lost you to your thoughts again." Annie smirks then gently grabs my arm to draw my attention to her. "Can I ask you something?"

"Always."

"If Reid were to tell you right now that he has a date with someone else tomorrow, what would you feel? After all, you two are just friends, right?"

I glance to see that Reid and Oscar are talking to the man offering a bowl of candy, which means I have a little time to answer. "He isn't tied down to me. We are friends, and I would be happy for him."

"Bullshi—hey, you two." Annie turns her attention to Oscar running toward us with Reid towing behind.

"I got Butterfingers." Oscar holds up his basket proudly.

I investigate his basket, full of enough candy. "A perfect way to end the evening. We should head home, as it's super cold. Plus, we need to hand out candy at our house too, you can help."

Immediately Oscar groans. "But we still have those houses to do." He points across the street.

"But Aunt Annie is freezing, and I really need to check on the candy." I run my hand through Oscar's hair.

"Want me to take him?" Reid offers.

My head immediately perks up in his direction and I see that he doesn't seem to mind. "Oh, you don't have to be dragged along."

"It's cool. We'll do a few more houses then come home."

"Are you sure? This isn't what I meant by tag along trick-or-treating with us." I feel bad, but I don't. I trust Reid with Oscar, and it helps me out by avoiding Oscar frowning for the next hour.

Reid reaches out to touch my shoulder, his eyes soft when they meet my own. "I promise. I might steal a candy bar, but hazards of the job, right?" He bobs his head to the side.

"Right." My upper lip twitches from the delight dancing around us.

Our no-contact embrace is broken when Oscar grabs Reid's arm. "Come on!" Oscar's tone is persistent.

"Just call me if you need something."

Reid is already getting pulled away. "Sure."

Annie's tongue clucks in her mouth as she hooks her arm around my shoulders to walk us back in the direction of my house. "I think I just felt my ovaries explode watching that. He cares about you."

"He's just helping," I protest. Truthfully, it is a little daunting seeing that Reid is, well, a kids type of person now. Add that to the positive traits list that I should not be keeping.

"Or trying to win points, but I don't know. You two have some quite sensual looks happening."

I try to brush it all out of my head. Impossible. But at least five minutes later, when I have a glass of wine in my hand and have refilled the candy bowl, I do feel calmer.

"It will all be okay. I know I don't get both. It's either the passion or the man who cares too much and may lack the passion. And since it's amazing sex then that is my sign that it needs to end because I don't get all the other stuff too." I speak aloud as if a tangent of thoughts wants to spew out of my head.

Annie stops examining the bottle of wine. "That is the craziest thing you've ever said. I think you really need to have a chat with the guy."

I nervously drink from my wine. "Mmhmm, totally right. I will talk to him."

"I'll watch Oscar in the morning before my flight. You can go meet Reid and do what you kids do to confuse your lives." Annie sips from her glass.

I tap the counter, breathing out a breath, knowing very well that I need to take Annie up on her offer.

For the next few minutes, we have a couple more kids at the door, but it's dying down. By the time Reid returns with Oscar, my son willingly goes to the sofa to flop down and watch some television, as he's exhausted.

I throw a blanket on Oscar and kneel down, picking up his pumpkin. "Let me investigate this stash, then you can have one piece before bedtime in half an hour."

"Okay, Mom, but don't eat my Butterfinger."

"Wouldn't dream of it." I ruffle his hair with my fingers.

Reid has a glass of wine and stands next to the counter with Annie. I pour the contents of the pumpkin onto the counter, and we all study the candy.

"Looks legit to me," Annie comments.

I grab a box of gummies and begin to attack it. "Completely, and he hates these, so they're mine."

"I have to say that it's kind of crazy seeing you both in the same room after all these years. Watch this one for me." Annie throws a thumb in my direction. "She can cook a mean lasagna, and I know it won't be long before someone wants her number to romance her. I'm sure you can assess if they have good intentions or not, *friend*." She smiles but the undertone of her sentence is enough to make me feel like this was a bad idea, to have us all under one roof.

Reid takes it in good stride, but I notice he adjusts his neck slightly. "Absolutely."

Luckily, for the next half-hour, we are able to talk about things to do in Chicago, and Annie tells us about her upcoming presentation for a research group she managed. When it's time for Oscar to go to bed, Annie offers to help him get ready, and Reid mentions that he's heading out.

"I'll walk you to the door," I offer.

I slide my glass of wine to the side and follow him, stopping when he waves goodbye to Oscar, and then we resume our journey. When the door opens, I feel equal parts disappointment that he's leaving and excitement, as if we are a step closer to an unknown destination.

He soothes me with strokes of his fingertips up my arm. "Enjoy catching up with Annie."

"I will. Thank you for stopping by. I guess we're even on the surprise-visitor front."

"Why, did you have plans if it was just you and me?" He's trying to coax me or entice me, all easy to do.

I feel my face turn warm, and I glance down at his hand on me. "I guess I would have offered for you to stay and watch a movie or something."

"Something," he echoes in a gruff voice.

I really wish I had more faith in divine intervention, as right now my thoughts are too impure and I need a rescue. I feel my body tingle in need for him to touch me, hold me, kiss me, as if it's the only thing that will end this confusion.

"Thanks for inviting me. I haven't gone trick-or-treating, well, I don't think since I was a kid. Goes on the list of all the things I wasn't expecting lately."

The corner of my mouth tugs. "I guess we have a habit of doing that to one another lately. Unexpected things."

He steps closer, and our bodies align, only an inch apart. I can feel his breath, smell his scent, and I swear I can sense his pulse. Reid breathes in my hair as my hands hang by my sides and our fingertips touch. "Good night." His lips nuzzle along my forehead, and I feel like my entire center has lost gravity.

Then I remember. "Tomorrow." The word falls off my tongue. "Annie will be with Oscar; can I stop by?"

A soft grunt sounds from the back of his throat. "I hope you do."

My heart is hammering at my chest, and his eyes make it feel as though he's hunting me. When he steps back, I know that tomorrow can't come soon enough.

14

LENA

Before I have a chance to knock, Reid opens the door, and we stare at one another. He's in jeans and a t-shirt, I'm in a skirt with tights and a sweater.

"Morning." I hold up a bag of bagels.

"Morning." He looks hungry and not for the food.

I feel my heart pounding in my chest.

One. Two. Three.

In a flash, he pulls me inside, the bag dropping to the floor. I hear the door close behind me, and I see nothing, as I close my eyes to enjoy his lips on my own, starting a fire inside of me.

I'm tugging at his shirt, and he's sliding my coat off. We circle and take a waltz of steps, as we have no sense of direction.

"This isn't why I came here," I whisper in between kisses, but I continue to let my hands explore his body. It's fervent, chaotic, and I'm starving. I kiss his neck as he yanks off my clothing.

"Shh. Let me get more of you," he murmurs against my mouth.

We continue to make our way to his room, with items of fabric landing on the floor. I jump up onto him, now only in our underwear. I kiss him hard, as if I want to punish him for leading me down this path, but in truth I'm just as much a willing participant as he is.

Reid's hands squeeze my ass as he spins us around, causing me to hold onto him tightly by pulling him closer to me, with my arms looped around his neck.

"I brought breakfast," I muse in between our kisses.

"Fuck that. There is only one thing that we should be doing right now."

We fall onto the bed, on our sides, my leg hooking over his hip while his mouth skims down my throat, then when he reaches my breasts, he darts his tongue out to tease me.

But there is something I want, and I shift my body until his cock is in the perfect position for me to get a taste.

Reid rubs a hand over his face as he groans. "You're my undoing."

"Debatable."

I start pulling down his boxer briefs, and he finishes the task so I focus my attention on his hard tip. I swirl my tongue around him, and I am beginning to wonder if he is a poisonous apple because I know this is everything that I shouldn't want.

Yet I take more and more. I stroke his length by holding his base and gliding my tongue along in different patterns from root to tip, licking his taste before taking him deeper into my mouth. I'm angled perfectly so his hands can roam around my body where I'm lying next to him as I enjoy him. The circles he rubs on my ass are soothing, but his hands are even better when they weave through my hair as my head bobs.

I suck him and lick, and my mouth waters from my

actions. I peer up at him, and I take satisfaction that his eyes are hooded closed and he's enjoying this moment.

"Lena," he moans with a thick breath.

Pulling off him, I slither my body up until our eyes meet; I need to be closer to him. The faintest of smiles stretches on his mouth, and he reaches his hand between us to touch me and make me needier to have him inside me.

I gasp into his neck as he slows when he finds the perfect spot to play with me. I part my thighs open, and he moves to bring himself closer, his cock finds home, and when he enters it still gives me an euphoria of surprise and pleasure.

We kiss as he moves deeper, our bodies tight together in an embrace. I move my pelvis to meet his thrusts, and he continues to devour my mouth and neck while he pins my wrists against the mattress.

"This way now. On your stomach later while I take you from behind. I need you coming all morning," he taunts, with his breath against my ear and his hand gripping my hair slightly.

"Shh. Just get us lost right now," I croon.

He nods before tilting his body deep into me, and I whimper from the way he takes me, but it's still a way that I could get addicted to. Reid has no remorse for taking me a little rough, partly because it's our method of communication. Avoid the obvious, and instead, move together while we make one another dizzy and insane.

We both feel our freefall approaching, and I reach between my legs to rub my clit as Reid's pace picks up.

"Ladies first." He gives me a devilish look before he stills inside of me to prevent his own orgasm and focuses with his fingers and his mouth on my nipples.

I dig my foot into his taut ass to gain some balance, and our foreheads touch as our eyes remain fixed on one another.

I feel my peak approaching, and only when I begin to tremble does Reid move again, riding a wave with me, my walls clenching around him as I come undone, and it doesn't take long for him to follow behind.

And then we lie there tangled in one another, both with pulses pumping at full speed.

I crawl my fingers up the skin on his upper arm, along his shoulder, to his neck, then landing on his bottom lip. This isn't a fantasy; I can touch him. I look at him with curiosity, and he just gazes back at me with warmth as he combs hair behind my ear.

We just lie here, unable to move, for what feels like ages. Lost in a moment that I'm not sure we should be having.

"I'm still inside of you," he whispers, and his grin informs me that he likes that very much.

The corner of my mouth twitches. "I guess I can't get far then."

He leans in to brush his lips along my own, before firmly planting a kiss on my mouth. I return as much as he gives, but we're soft. As if we are simmering together in a pot of confusion or a spell that has possessed us.

Pulling away, our eyes connect in recognition, a simple fact that I confirm. "We can't lie like this all day."

"A shame." He caresses my cheek in his palm. "Your skirt when it hits the floor makes a sound. I like it."

I give him a peculiar look. "It doesn't make a sound."

"It does, and it reminds me that I'm undressing you."

I swallow and drag my fingers along his collarbone. "I like the sound when you unbuckle your belt. It reminds me that you're going to take me."

"I like that." He grins proudly then taps my hip, indicating that I should unhook from him. The moment he slides out of me, I feel a loss that it's the end of this moment. He kisses a line down my thigh to my knee before leaving the bed.

When he goes to the bathroom, I sit up to search for the clothes that did make it to the bedroom, and it doesn't give me many options, so I don't leave my position. Instead, I fall back and let my fingers draw along my stomach like a feather to touch myself, to ensure I haven't left earth.

When Reid returns with a cloth, he grabs hold of my knee to part me open, and then he hovers over me and cleans me up with the cloth. Our eyes never blink or part. This whole action is an intimate reminder that we find ourselves always entangled, especially as I rest my arms over my head with my body on display for him.

His eyes skim over me, and he groans softly in approval right before he throws the cloth to the side to lie on the bed next to me. Reid's fingers land on my skin, and he teases me by circling along my hip.

But I'm smarter than that.

"What are we doing?" I ask, with my eyes wistful.

"Relaxing a moment before I make you brunch then insist you ride me."

Gah, his fingers move so affectionately.

I give a pointed look. "I brought bagels, so I think I made brunch, *and* you know what I mean."

Reid's jaw flexes, and he seems to be thinking of how to answer. "Enjoying one another." He sounds honest, at least.

I take in his words, and I feel a familiar flame ignite inside of me. It causes me to roll off the bed and grab my panties off the floor. Every move is extra sharp because I feel emotions, a lot of familiar emotions.

It's a mixture of déjà vu, like a jar opening that housed everything I once felt then buried.

Reid also leaves the bed. "Lena, what is it?" he innocently asks and finds his clothes too.

"I came here to talk, I think we should talk, so let's—"

"Talk." He's trying to be funny.

It frustrates me, and I walk out of the room, following the trail of our bad idea on the floor, with Reid not far behind me. But it wasn't even a bad idea, because sex with him is perfect, mind-boggling, and I don't have the will to regret it.

Grabbing my bra, I struggle to clasp it back on. Reid steps behind me and slowly helps, but it sends a shiver across my chest because his touch somehow possesses me to want more; it's a talent he's always had.

He lingers and rests his hand on my shoulder causing me to feel anchored. "What are we doing?" I softly repeat my earlier question with my back to him.

"In general, or my current plans? I was going to convince you not to put on another scrap of clothing." His tone is serious, which causes me to turn to meet his gaze, but I'm not impressed. Reid steps back and seems to be pondering his thoughts. "I'm not sure."

"Me neither, but I do know one thing. You've somehow managed to stay in my life all these years, even if you had no idea. A constant problem in my head."

"You've mentioned."

"With you it was always so incredibly passion-driven. We were…"

He squints one eye. "Sexually compatible? Yeah."

I glance to the side then back to him because his stare is tense. "It also taught me that amazing passion doesn't equate love. You didn't love me, nor did you want a relationship beyond whatever we were doing."

"Not then, no," he answers simply.

A sound of disappointment escapes me. "Sometimes I think I

compared every other relationship with the way you and I were physically, and there was no comparison. But then I remembered we were probably that way because we were nothing else."

"That's how you formed your theory that you can't have both? Great sex and a guy who loves you?"

I nod in agreement. "It took me a long time to get over you. A very long time. When I got married, I thought it was finally okay, because in the end I ended up with who I probably should be with, all the boxes checked, even if the passion wasn't the same. But that didn't work out, and now you are back in my life. But I'm wiser now, Reid. I won't make the same mistake twice," I warn him.

His tongue circles inside of his mouth as his hands land on his hips. "Let me get this straight, you are assuming I'm just like I was then? Lena, I'm not twenty-two anymore." There is disapproval in his voice.

"I'm guarding my heart because I know you've changed, and I'm not sure what that means for me. I just need to keep my caution based on the past. It's not just me now. I'm a package deal with a little guy who can't have his mom making a stupid mistake."

Reid raises his head in attention, then steps closer to me again. He grips my shoulders to ensure that I look him straight in the eye. "Is that what you think we're doing? Just messing around for fun?"

I scoff a laugh. "It's not like we're doing much more."

His eyes bug out at me. "What was last night?"

"Trick-or-treating?" I'm puzzled.

"Yeah. You let me be around your son."

I shrug.

"My world has been pretty small lately, until you waltzed back in," he tells me.

"All the more reason we should probably not mess up the friendship we could have. If that's even possible," I mutter the last part to myself.

Reid drags his hand across his face. He doesn't seem pleased with my words, but one of us has to be smart about all of this.

"You're pushing me away?" he asks.

I notice my sweater on the floor and grab it to pull over my head. "I don't know what I'm doing, I never do when I'm around you. That hasn't changed. But we need to do better if we have any hope of not causing an explosion that doesn't end well for one of us."

Reid slowly nods his head in understanding. "I get it." He sounds somber, but he can't resist and reaches out to cup my cheek and rub the pad of his thumb along my skin. I take the opportunity to breathe him in and feel the warmth of his hand.

"Stay longer?"

I shake my head gently. "I need to get home, and already talking to you while you stand shirtless before me is testing my restraint," I attempt to joke.

"Is this you telling me to give you space or you telling me that I need to figure it out?" he wonders.

"It's your turn to find that answer. You're smart, Professor." I dab my finger against his chest. "I've said my piece and know my boundaries, and it's hard, but I think I'm doing the right thing."

I notice his Adam's apple bob as he swallows, maybe even nervously. "When I discover our answer?"

I give him a closed half-smile. "Bring me pumpkin pie and tell me about it."

He leans down to kiss my forehead, tenderly and long-

ingly. When we part, we look at one another in acknowledg-
ment that this is the right thing to do.

It still doesn't make it any easier when I walk out his
door, but I feel at peace because it just means I can't get in
any deeper now.

15

REID

Walking from the parking lot, I debate with myself if this is a good idea. But Prudence sent a reminder that she has a stall at the Hollows Fall Festival, and when I mentioned a special winery would also have a stall, then Johnny was sold to become my partner in crime.

Johnny nudges my arm as we enter the festival area in front of the courthouse. It's afternoon, crowded, a bit nippy in temperature, and I've been in a mood for a week or two.

"Fresh air will be good for you," he informs me for the fifth time today.

"I went for a run this morning," I remind him.

He chuckles under his breath. "I haven't seen you with your lady friend in a while."

"Lena and I are just friends."

"I'm not deaf, I heard you the other week at ten in the morning."

I look at him skeptically because Lena and I weren't *that* loud. Then again, I was too focused on staring into her eyes as I made her come. "Let's get some mulled wine or something." I indicate in the direction of the Olive Owl stall, thankful I can replenish my supply, as they have bottles on sale and their winery is about an hour away.

"Why are you being so stubborn? Just romance her over dinner."

I touch my short beard. "That's not the problem. The issue is that I shouldn't do that unless I'm certain that I won't hurt her."

"But sometimes you need to test the waters, otherwise you won't know."

I listen to him as I indicate for two cups of warm cider— the adult version—then add two bottles of white to bring home. Why did I just choose white? Probably because subconsciously I'm thinking of Lena and what she would drink if I invited her over.

"We aren't new to one another; it's not about testing the waters. It's… understanding what I feel because it isn't like it was then," I admit as I pay the guy who I can only assume is one of the three brothers that own the winery.

Johnny and I hold our drinks and continue our slow walk, exploring a mix of fall goodies and a few people trying to sell Christmas decorations. Up ahead I see Prudence and her stall, and I nod my head to greet her when she takes notice of me.

"Lucky Hollows residents, we have two good-looking gentlemen walking around." She smiles as she straightens a candle on display.

"How are the customers today?" I ask her as I study the options in her stall.

She quirks her lips out. "Can't complain. I'm pushing the candles and lavender for sleeping. It's great that you both stopped by."

"The other option is he sits at home, listens to records,

and drowns his sorrows in a whiskey glass," Johnny gladly explains my life as of late.

"No," I say, quick to defend. "Probably would just have graded assignments or something." I shrug.

Prudence brings a hand to her hip. "I'm surprised you're not here with Lena."

My face has a hardened look due to hearing Lena's name, and Prudence instantly looks to Johnny for an answer.

"It's getting a little confusing," he offers in answer to explain my relationship status.

"I'm sure you'll figure it out. She's good for your aura, I picked it up when you both came into my store. She brings you light. Anyway, I'm positive I've seen her around here." Her eyes grow wide.

I look around as if Lena will suddenly appear. "Here?" I point to the ground.

"Yeah."

"Right, with her son." I try to throw logic into the equation.

Prudence shakes her head. "Nope."

I stiffen slightly and rub the back of my neck. Of course she would be here, as she loves autumn, and this whole event celebrates crunchy leaves and the smell of nutmeg. Over the last day, I debated texting her because this is exactly the kind of event I would take her to as a friend or more. Instead, I opted for maturity and not confusing us.

"Want some herbs? To cleanse your mind? Awaken your heart?" she offers with a pointed look.

At least it causes me to break out in a grin. "I don't need any of that. Maybe me overthinking this is the sign that it's not going to work, you know?"

Johnny chuckles, and he exchanges a glance with Prudence. "Or it could be the absolute opposite. You mentioned it yourself, that you feel different this time, and maybe your body is in shock that, at last, you could end up with who you were meant to be with."

"Now you are ready for one another," Prudence adds her two cents before turning her attention to a customer.

My heart tugs at that thought, in a favorable way too.

"Lena! Small world," Johnny calls out.

My head whips in the direction of his line of sight, and Lena is a beautiful image. She has a cute-as-fuck beanie hat on her head as she walks toward us with a shy smile.

"Hey, Johnny. Small town, small festival, what are the chances?" She finds this coincidence amusing. Her eyes land on me, and she attempts to maintain her soft smile.

I mouth *hello* because when our eyes connect, I'm suddenly not capable of speaking. But then I blink and quickly throw a question out. "Where's Oscar?" I look behind her to see nobody trailing behind.

"With a friend. Only a few weeks at school and already getting invited over for playdates. He's in demand." Her polite smile doesn't fade.

"That's great." I'm happy for her, as she was worried about him adapting. "I'm sure you will need a separate calendar to keep track of Oscar's busy social schedule."

Everyone around us may as well disappear because the world feels like it's stopped.

"You thought you would check out your new favorite celebration?"

She nods. "Yeah, there's someone selling yarn, and I thought I would attempt to make a scarf or something. Keep my hands busy."

When her eyes stall, I realize that she let it slip that she has a reference imprinted in her head of how to use her hands in other ways. It causes me to smirk.

"You're here alone?" I wonder.

"No. I'm supposed to be meeting a colleague who is fast becoming a friend. We were going to take advantage of Oscar being at a friend's and try the new brewery for a drink."

"Oh. That's..." A disappointment, as I was hoping to prolong this surprise encounter.

The clearing of a throat draws our attention to Johnny. "You know, Prudence could use a hand here. I think I'll stay put for a little bit." Johnny gives me the eye.

Grabbing my opportunity, I quickly jump in. "Sounds good." I look back at Lena. "Can I walk with you until your friend comes?"

She rolls her lips in as she smiles to herself. "Sure."

Prudence, who is still with a customer, doesn't notice, and I give Johnny a confirmation with my eyes that I'll be back.

The moment Lena and I are walking side by side, I feel the pull to bring her closer. Not just now, either.

"I feel like this place is a fantasy," she comments as she looks around.

"They put on a good show, huh?"

"What's Christmas like?"

I let our arms touch. "Well, it's all the seasonal holidays, so a mix of celebrations, and it's quite possible the number of lights may cause the entire state's electrical grid to crash."

She stops and turns to me with a wide smile. "And this is where you ended up drinking gingerbread lattes and teaching students?"

"And here you are in the same place."

It feels like there's a magnet keeping us close to one another, yet we don't touch; we continue to walk, unable to keep our distance.

"You had a good week?"

"It was okay, and you?"

I scoff. "Same old, same old. Students who piss me off and impress me all in one go, my mother calling every day, and I should probably cut the caffeine." She nods in understanding, but I want more, and I touch her arm to stop our stroll, which surprises her. "The thing is... that life kind of sucks. I had a shitty few years thanks to cancer and a fiancée who I thought I loved. I've been turning the wheels of life ever since. But then—"

Her finger lands on my mouth to shush me. "Don't say it," she warns me. "Don't confuse lust with something else. Or the fact we have a history, so it's easy to get attached to the familiar."

I pull her finger away and gently keep hold of it and slide my fingers to her wrist. "I know. You made your point clear that I should think about the bigger picture."

"Good." Lena stands taller.

"I'm not going to hurt you," I promise, and my tone is serious. "I want to do right by you."

We both stand and stare, with a silence looming around us.

She tries to avoid my gaze. "Apple butter. I saw a stall for that, should probably check that out." She attempts to steer our conversation in another direction.

"Avoidance much?"

She rolls her eyes at me and smirks, and I'm relieved we can insert ease into the conversation. I let her wrist go so we can continue to stroll along the line of stalls, and I appreciate how much I enjoy this. Just walking, watching, and breathing in the air. But undoubtedly, it's having Lena next to me that I know is causing me the most bliss.

"Want to know something funny?" she asks.

"Surprise me."

"I was at the grocery store and there were two girls

picking out ice cream, along with their cans of White Claw, and they were talking about this mean professor who has been grumpy all week, but they'll allow it because he has searing eyes worth every 9am lecture."

I smirk to myself. "Let me guess. The mean yet good-looking professor was me?"

She shrugs her shoulder. "I mean, they never mentioned names, but I think we know you are the prime suspect."

"Will you ever surprise me again in my lecture?"

She laughs. "No way. I was mesmerized for the hour but have zero interest in what you talk about."

"Oh, thanks." I slide my hands into my pockets.

Now she gives me the taunting look. "Uh-oh, did I offend you? Someone actually doesn't want to follow your class?"

"Nah, it's okay. I can handle it. I'm sure my lectures to you are the equivalent of your knitting skills to me," I tease her and immediately she pinches me. "Ouch. You have a claw there."

I grab her wrist again, and we find ourselves in an awkward yet intimate position where her eyes peer up at me, and if I moved an inch then I could capture her mouth. And I want to.

"Thank you," she whispers.

I have no clue why she says that. "What for?"

"Making me laugh. I needed that for so many reasons."

"Am I a reason?" I thread my fingers through the end of her strands of hair.

"Yeah… you are." Then her smirk widens. "Not necessarily for the right reason."

I want to kiss her, but she isn't mine to kiss, not yet anyway. "Lena…"

She pats my shoulders before breaking our embrace. "I

see my friend. I need to go. It was good to see you." I hear the sincerity in her tone.

"Yeah… you too." I reluctantly drop her arm as she vanishes faster than a shooting star.

I curse to myself as I watch her head into the distance. I take a breather before I return to the stall where both Prudence and Johnny are giving me a stern look.

"That was some sexual tension," Prudence blankly says before holding out a stick of herbs. "For your aura. It might need some clarifying because you seem to have a blockage between your heart and mind."

"No shit." I'm frustrated with myself and grab the stick because all options are on the table to get me out of this mood.

Johnny just shakes his head at me. "You get one life, kid. Don't think for too long. You more than anyone knows how it can change in a second. You survived for a reason, so grasp on to your second chance at happiness."

I nod in understanding before getting on with the day, with a secret hope that I'll run into Lena again.

16

REID

A week later, I'm lying awake and burning some patchouli incense while I listen to music. But I can't resist, and I call Lena. I wait for her to pick up as I pace my living room and stop in front of a plant to study the leaves.

"Hey." She sounds tired.

"Hey... sorry, did I wake you?"

"No, it's okay. I had a long day, so as soon as Oscar went to bed, I took a bath and I'm now binging a show in bed," she explains.

I turn my head away from the phone and bite my fist because the image is playing in my head. It takes all my power not to ask what she's wearing.

Clearing my throat, I remember I called her for a reason. "I just wanted to check if you're around for Thanksgiving. I'm not sure in our current state if this is allowed, but I'm not heading to my parents', and Johnny has a big dinner if you have no plans."

"That's... nice of you to offer, but Oscar is going to

Sean's parents', and a colleague invited me to dinner in the city."

"Right. Good. I mean, sounds like you have plans."

She scoffs a sound on the other end. "Is that really why you called?"

I let down my defenses. "No. Truthfully, I wanted to hear your voice, and I know asking you to turn on the video chat would land me in the doghouse."

"Only if I'm wearing my short black nightdress."

My brows raise. "I'm not allowed to ask if you are, am I?"

I can hear her smile by the change of her breath. "Is there something else?"

"I hate this," I admit. "Not having you next to me in bed, even if it's for a moment, talking with you over coffee, sending messages about ridiculous things. I'm not avoiding you, I'm avoiding the answer, because I don't have it in me to hurt you twice in this lifetime." Quickly I realize that she may take it the wrong way. "Shit." I pinch the bridge of my nose between my fingers. "I mean, it's not that I don't want to be with you, I just know this time it's different, and I won't give you an answer until I know I can fully commit."

"Maybe you never will, Reid. I think I'm going to hang up. This conversation isn't helping anyone, and I need to get up early. Good night."

She hangs up before I can explain further.

I groan and collapse onto my sofa, and immediately the memory of her laughing in my arms after breakfast on this very couch comes to me.

I've never overthought something so much, but then, as I stare at the ceiling, it dawns on me that I've been wallowing for too long. Especially when it isn't a situation at all, it's fate throwing me a wild card or a gift because the answer has been with me all this time. Buried deep, but it was there.

It's clear as day what has me afraid to give an answer.

The full commitment.

I'm taking my time because I know a commitment with Lena is probably the last one I'll make in my life because there will be nobody else. She's the one.

———

THE NEXT DAY, I find myself at Lena's house, sitting on a step waiting for her.

I remember that Oscar was going to his grandparents', and Lena was going to a colleague's for dinner. And thank the fuck for American football and planning Thanksgiving dinner around the football schedule, which means everyone eats early in the day. Because it's seven pm and I'm waiting for Lena to walk up the path. The moment she does, she stalls when she approaches me, unsure why I'm here.

"Have a nice Thanksgiving?" I wonder.

She shrugs a shoulder up to her ear. "It was nice... just not the same as most years. You?"

"I was with Johnny and his family. It was... just missing someone." I stand and debate if I should just jump in. "This isn't how either one of us should be celebrating your favorite holiday, I guess." I step closer, and I don't let her speak because my pulse is in my ears, and I need to get this out. "I have a theory."

"Reid, what are you doing here?" She looks around as if this is some prank, before crossing her arms to keep warm because it's freezing out. The streetlight highlights our faces, which gives her a warm glow, and even I can see her eyes glazed with hope.

I hold up a box from the grocery store. "I was supposed to bring you a pumpkin pie when I figured out our answer."

"Oh?" She seems nervous. "What's that?"

"I think in life we have the opportunity to fall in love twice. Sometimes with two different people, sometimes the same person, at different times. I don't know, but I believe back then you weren't the one for me and I fell for someone else. But it was meant to be that way because you were meant for me now when I'm quite possibly a better person."

She lowers her head and doesn't seem happy about my theory. "Reid, this…"

"Think about it. You were supposed to be with Oscar's father. You made a child with him, and now you can love someone else, because you and I were quite possibly always going to find one another." She scoffs a bitter laugh, and I don't understand, as it all made sense in my head. "You can have it all, Lena. The incredible sex, the guy who cares, the relationship that maybe you've been preparing for your whole life. Maybe I've been preparing for it too." I step closer to her which causes her body to perk up in attention. "We didn't get it right with someone else, but we don't regret that. You don't leave my mind, the only thing that makes sense lately is having you in my life."

"But as what?"

I tilt my head to the side. "Do you want to go out next week? There is this indoor trampoline park that I'm sure Oscar would love."

"As in a date?" She's confused.

"Yeah," I answer.

Her arms fall to her sides, and she breathes a long exhale. "Reid, don't ask things unless you know what you're signing up for. It's all or nothing."

"Tell me what that looks like then," I request.

I can tell her body is running on adrenaline. "It's going slow. Snail's-pace slow. Romantic dinners, the kind you never asked me on before. No sleepovers until Oscar knows who you are in my life. And that only happens if we are certain we're in it for the long haul. It looks like logistical planning around when I have Oscar and when I don't. It involves awkward first meetings with my ex because he needs to know who is in Oscar's life. And then one day maybe we will move in together if you can handle my crappy knitting skills, my new addiction to burning sage, and a boy who is number one in my life. It's not easy. It's complicated, it's scary as hell, but that's maybe what excites us the most."

A long silence takes over as I register everything she just said. I can see her chest nearly heaving by the movement of her scarf around her coat because she's nervous, and fuck, I don't want to hurt her. My mind quickly runs through the list she just presented to make sure I'm making the right decision, the decision I made already weeks ago but couldn't admit aloud.

I stall for a moment and our eyes hold.

"So, would next Sunday work for the trampoline park?" I ask again.

Her mouth begins to form a smile.

17

LENA

Reid looks at me with a fixed smirk because he knows he has me. I pull my coat tighter around my body, my breath visible in the night air, and I try to keep my smile from spreading uncontrollably.

But the fact he's staring at me has me under his magic as I stride once toward him. "So, about that pie," I say.

He knows I'm teasing him by not giving him an answer. Reid groans as he steps closer to me, his free arm looping around my middle to pull me abruptly to him. I reach up to play with the lapels of his coat, distracting me from the fact that it feels like so many moments have led us on a long journey to this scene. It's a dream that never left me, even if I buried it.

"I'm not going anywhere." His voice sounds determined.

My eyes flick up to meet his. "I don't want you to," I confirm. Leaning up on my toes, I wrap my arms around his neck, and he meets me halfway for a kiss, the kind that steals my breath and sears my lips. It's powerful and only heightened by the fact he pulls me up against his body, leaving my feet to dangle before setting me down again.

When he pulls away, he places popcorn kisses on my lips, my chin, cheek, everywhere.

"I kept thinking about what I would do if you had the answer I wanted. I wasn't sure if this is a route I should go down at this moment in time, for Oscar or maybe even me. But it didn't feel right, that idea, because it wouldn't matter, you always linger in my mind. And you're right, I think we weren't meant to be then, but now we have no excuse because we may just be everything we were waiting for."

He leans his forehead in to touch my own. "You're mine, and I'll be damned if I let you go this time."

"That's good because you have pumpkin pie and that's quite critical for this evening," I quip. Offering my hand, we head inside.

It takes a few moments to turn the lights on and get our coats off, but it takes only a second for his hand to land back on my body as we walk to the kitchen. Of course, he chooses my lower back just above my ass as the destination for his hand, and all the while he leans in to kiss my neck as he walks by my side.

My smile doesn't fade, even when we nearly drop the pie. In fact, we carelessly throw it on the counter, right before he hoists me up and plants me on the marble surface. He steps between my knees, causing my thighs to part. Then his mouth is on my lips again, and I just can't get enough, but we have time. My fingertips land on his chest to create distance.

He studies me with his elated look as I lean and reach into the drawer to grab two forks, then quickly hand him one.

"Don't want to save the pie for a post-makeup-sex snack?" He raises a brow at me.

I shake my head firmly but still my grin doesn't falter. "No. We should kind of talk before that happens."

Reid's face softens, and the corners of his lips twist in

understanding. We clink our forks together before diving into the pie.

"I'm not sure I'm even hungry, but it feels like this is how we should commemorate the evening," I reflect.

"I could think of other ways, but sure, a little more sugar today is exactly what we should enjoy." I hear the lack of enthusiasm for that theory in his voice, but I only find it entertaining.

We both take a bite of the pie, and I notice his eyes focus on something behind me. I glance over my shoulder to see a block tower that Oscar built the other day, and it's not to be touched, per his orders.

Looking back at Reid, I highlight the obvious. "Yep, I have a son, remember?" I remind him and wonder if this is where he freaks out about what he's signing up for.

"I know." He takes another scoop of pie.

"Okay, just so we are clear, toys scattered around are kind of a bonus when you decide that I'm the one you want to start something with."

He smiles to himself as if he was prepared that I may gently grill him. "I know, and it's not a deterrent."

Butterflies move around my chest again. This is happening, it's really happening.

I grab his fork and place it to the side along with mine before I interlace our hands, leaning in to nuzzle my nose with his own. "We're doing this. Slow."

"Yes." He skims his lips along the corners of my mouth. "But not for tonight."

In one movement, he slides me off the counter, and I instantly wrap my legs around his waist while our lips simultaneously fuse together.

He carries me, and without asking for directions, he finds my room, and we fall onto my bed together, lying across the mattress horizontally and nowhere near a pillow, but it doesn't matter. We're quick to discard clothing, and I don't get much chance to admire his naked body because he's between my legs, rubbing his tip between my folds.

"Fuck, you're ready," he comments against the skin of my breast.

"It doesn't take much from you, now take me," I insist.

He trails his lips up and down my throat, back to my mouth, then I feel his hand reach between us, flicking my clit a few times before guiding his length inside of me. Instantly, I dig my nails into his back because he goes deep. The way I like it when we have confirmations to make.

"Harder," I implore.

"Wrap your legs tighter around me, I want to get deeper," he insists with a gravelly voice.

I comply and feel new sensations inside of me. I tilt my pelvis up to get more because I'm greedy in this moment.

We fuck with abandon, and our breaths are laced with moans. And when he pins my wrists to the mattress next to my head then looks me in the eyes, I have an inclination that a part of me was always with him, and I get it back in this very moment. It's crazy but every sign is indicating that this is right, what it's supposed to be.

I like who I am now, I like who he is, and most of all, we are better now than then.

I tip my lips up to capture a kiss and our sounds mix between our mouths, the mattress moving with us on every thrust.

God, when we both get there, I think we evaporate into the mattress, unable to move, and it doesn't even matter because we are together with twisted limbs, and my favorite part is when he rests his chin into the curve of my neck, not leaving me.

"I can't get enough of you," he mumbles against my lips.

I comb my fingers through his hair. "That's good because you're stuck with me. We have a lot to figure out, but you are so stuck with me."

"In that case, let's sleep like this. We did it once."

I hum in response. "I remember, the superpowers of the younger us. We fell asleep with you inside of me and woke and you were still inside of me. I didn't think it was physically possible."

"It's only possible with you and..." He begins to stir and then I realize he is rolling us until he's on his back. "We're trying it again."

I cuddle into him tighter, resting my ear against his heart. I can hear the beat, strong and steady and finally for me.

18

LENA

—

Walking into Ginger & Co., I feel my mouth stretch when I see Reid who is standing with his feet firmly planted with no intention of going anywhere as he studies the menu.

"We're really doing this? You haven't changed your mind yet?" I drop my arms and step closer to him.

He glances to me, and his face has subtle vulnerability, as if he's afraid of my question, but his peaceful smirk tells me that he knows I'm happy to be here.

"Ordering an eggnog latte because pumpkin lattes have been kicked to the curb?"

I interlace our arms while we both look forward, and I sigh. "Technically it's the shortest day of the year, which means fall is over. They could have waited." There's disdain in my voice. "But I meant you and me, not the lattes."

Reid snorts a laugh due to my seasonal preference, then grows serious. "Yeah, we're doing this," he confirms. "I'm ready for you now." His statement confirms that he means it, and I still can't get enough of him confirming it. It's been nearly a month since he showed up at my door.

"This is a change from our first real date at the trampoline park." I have to poke the bear.

He tips his head to the side, and he hides his hand in his pocket. "I mean, I would have preferred a candlelit dinner, but figured I would get points if I included Oscar, and it shows commitment." And I appreciate it.

"We have an hour," I mention, and I give him a mischievous wink.

He turns to thread his fingers through my hair. "Better make it worth it then and let me kiss you."

I reach my arms up to circle around his neck, and he angles his mouth down to kiss me. And not just any kiss, it's us rooted to the ground for a future. He wraps his arm around my middle to pull me up and off the ground, flush to his body, and he twirls me around. His warmth spreads throughout my body and my heart wants to jump out of my chest. We both murmur indistinguishable sounds before he sets me back down as we get more from our kiss, drawing it out so it doesn't end.

Then when it does, his fingers immediately touch my cheek.

The clearing of a throat draws our attention to the barista who is shyly watching us. "Uhm, did you want to order?"

Reid and I chuckle softly at one another. "Yeah, sorry, we got carried away there. We're kind of new into this relationship, well, not really, but you know how it goes."

The barista who looks to be seventeen just smiles awkwardly. "I don't. Was it two eggnog lattes?" she answers, one-toned.

"Sure. Going to guess ginger plays a starring role," Reid quips. He pays, then we head to a table by the window to look out at the cold, snowy December day.

I take Reid's hand into my own. "Oscar was wondering why we haven't seen you in a while."

He looks at me, puzzled. "It's only been a few days since I've seen him. Remember, pizza, and then he went to sleep, and I ravished his mother before sneaking out."

"Sense of time is different for him."

We have been going slow, so Oscar still sees Reid as my friend who we hang out with every now and then. We've had a babysitter twice while Reid and I had a date, just the two of us, and Oscar didn't seem to connect any dots. But the last month feels like a rollercoaster that's accelerating us toward the finish line that we were meant for.

I shrug a shoulder and then smile brightly at the barista who delivers our drinks. Then frown when I look at the latte that is flavored with eggnog and not pumpkin.

"You can do this, I have faith," Reid encourages in a joking manner.

"I'm going to have to get through winter, so might as well," I declare before taking a sip. It isn't that bad—all right really, maybe even good.

Reid pulls our interlaced hands. "Out with the season of change and in with the season where I'm going to keep you warm at every opportunity."

I slide my chair closer to him. "Every opportunity?" I nuzzle into him, ready to get my flirt on.

He groans sinfully low in his throat before nipping his teeth against my cheek. "My mother decided to fly out for Christmas with my father."

"Wow, way to kill the mood," I joke. Maintaining my tight-lipped smile, I ask the obvious. "Is your mother's surprise visits an occurrence I should get used to?"

Reid pulls back with a devilish smirk before tapping my

nose. "Oh, you know it. But I promise, when we move in together one day, I won't give her a key."

"Wonderful." I slide my eyes away from his gaze. My heart jumps every time he talks about a future.

Funny silence dances around us, and I draw my attention back to Reid with a curious look on my face.

"They know," he confirms.

"About you and me?"

Reid nods as he drinks from his coffee and then sets his mug back down. "Call it my mother's sixth sense, and I couldn't deny it."

I wave him off. "It's no big deal. Another step for us."

"I like that." He quickly steals a kiss on my lips, before sinking back in the chair to enjoy the rest of his coffee. "Dealing with the eggnog latte okay?"

I study the contents in my hand. "I guess it's our second chance at love. I mean, I wasn't a fan of the drink before, but this time around... I don't know, maybe the latte and I have a thing now."

A smirk plays on Reid's lips. "Subtle."

"Might be a very large thing." I try to hide my laugh, but I can't because these are our days—constant smiles that keep us in an elated mood.

He's quick to tickle me and wraps his arm around my middle. Our eyes catch and we enjoy the moment between us.

Then he does my favorite thing and glides the pad of his thumb along my jawline, his gaze keeping me captive. "I love you," he whispers.

My face freezes as my entire heart jumps out of my chest, and surprise hits me in a wave. He's never said those words to me, and even when I felt long ago that I could say it, a fact hits me.

I now believe if I had told him how I felt all those years

ago, then it wouldn't feel the way it does in this very moment. It's completely right, as if the key clicks into a lock. And call me old-fashioned but he said it first which makes me feel even more confident and safe when I reply.

"I love you too."

Our lips search for one another and land in a perfect angle for a kiss to seal us together. The taste of coffee lingers on his lips, not pumpkin, but at least there is fucking nutmeg, ginger, and a hell of a lot of heart.

I guess winter won't be that bad.

EPILOGUE: REID

2 YEARS LATER

Dropping my keys onto the tray by the front door, I breathe in and recognize that the house is quiet. I take an extra-long inhale because I know what I am walking into. But this is what we want.

I head up the stairs and see that our bedroom door is slightly ajar. Should I knock or not? Nah, play it casual. It'll be less stressful for us all.

"Lena, I did the drop-off. Oscar is with his dad now for the weekend," I say as I enter the room. Then stop in my tracks when I see that the mood in our bedroom is completely different.

"I guess we got lucky with timing," she nervously tries to joke.

My eyes scan the scene before me. The lights are dim, candles all around, and I'm positive Lena burned some herbs from Prudence, and Lena is lying before me in dark green lace that shows a lot of cleavage that is damn distracting and may sidetrack us. Then there's the fact that the fabric barely covers the tops of her thighs, but that's the point.

I begin to unbutton my cufflinks as I survey Lena splayed out on the bed with her hips on a mountain of pillows. I took Oscar to his dad's while Lena took one of those test things that told us it's turkey baster time—her words, not mine.

Not going to lie, I may have hit the accelerator on my way home because we have a window of opportunity.

Rolling up my sleeves, I ask, "So, we're doing this?" I need to double-check, even though I know the answer.

Her eyes narrow in on me as she sits up on her propped elbows. "If you're on board then I'm ready." She smiles confidently and wiggles her fingers against the mattress.

I scoff a sound before a grin forms on my mouth. Because I'm not only on board, I'm leading the ship. I threw out the idea a few months ago because the idea of Lena carrying our child hasn't left my mind.

"Where's the treasure?" I ask, ready to play my part.

"In the bathroom. Remember how to do it?" she checks.

I laugh. "Yep, the doctor explained how I use the syringe to welcome my guys back into the world."

"Music or no music?" She squints her eyes in question.

I love how we're going all-in on setting the mood on the inseminating-my-girlfriend train. I'll add the ring to her finger later because we can't ruin this potential milestone moment, need to focus.

"I know you want to use the get-Lena-knocked-up playlist, so let's do it." I shake my head, entertained, before heading to the bathroom. I mean, we chose some good sensual tunes, so why not?

After getting everything in order, I return to the bedroom with items in one hand and arrive at the end of the bed. I kneel down by the edge then kiss a line up each thigh before I nuzzle my nose around her inner leg. I can feel her shiver and breathe deep.

"Nervous?"

She hums a sound. "No. But I'm not sure making me aroused is part of this."

"It can be." I use my free hand to rub warmth up her thigh to soothe her. "I have every intention of making you come today, it'll help open you up and welcome the swimmers in," I assure her.

Her lips purse out for another calming breath as she nods.

She props up her upper body. "Remember, if it doesn't work, we can try again."

"I know."

"And if it is a success, babies are a lot of work."

"I know," I state again.

She nibbles on her bottom lip. "Your mother doesn't know about this, right?"

I drop my head. "Wow, not the image I need in my head now. And no, it'll be our secret until it's official if we get lucky."

She flops back onto the mattress again. "Okay. Sorry, I guess I am a little nervous. It's my body that needs to do the work. This is what I want, but I don't want to fail you."

I hold her knee that is pointed toward the ceiling, as her feet are planted on the mattress. "You could never. The path will lead us."

She smiles warmly at me. "You're right. Now maybe remind me what you'll do later?" She bobs her head a little to the side.

"I'll lick you senseless then drive myself into you to fuck you so hard that I will hit your womb deep?" I raise my brows at her.

A sound of pleasure escapes her. "Yes, that's what I wanted to hear."

"You'll stay on your back and I'll do all the work. Take my time with you then fill you up in literally every way possible. You may be sore tomorrow from how much I'm going to worship your pussy today."

A moan escapes her. "Okay, we're good to go. I'm relaxed."

"Here we go," I announce. I grab the syringe in the cup, then hold it up to watch her cues. "Ready?"

She reaches forward to interlace with my free hand. I'm not going to let her tight grip go, not a chance.

"More than."

I tip my head down to kiss below her belly button. Bringing the important tool into position, I lock eyes with Lena as I slowly enter her.

"Deeper," she breathes. I follow the command. "Right there."

I watch her and she looks radiant. "I'm going to let it all go."

"This is kind of hot," she muses.

I smile softly and then take action, ensuring our two hands stay together. "I love you."

"I love you. Now kiss me," she demands.

Leaning down and hovering over her, I do just that. I would much rather attempt to get her pregnant another way, but this is probably the next best thing, and considering why we're in this situation, then I think we're lucky.

After pulling out of her, she stays put, and I set the things to the side. Lying next to her on my back, I rejoin our hands.

"Rest for half an hour and then I'm completely devouring you to orgasm. Then in a few hours we do this whole thing again." I place a soft kiss on her shoulder.

She turns her head in my direction. "I think I'm really going to enjoy today."

"Of course you are. It's Thanksgiving, and the stars have aligned so that it has to be today we try."

"Funny that coincidence, huh? My favorite time of year." She begins to circle her fingers along her womb.

"I have store-bought pumpkin pie in the fridge, ready for me to serve you at your beck and call."

She runs her fingers along my stubbled chin. "The best kind there is."

"Are you relaxed?"

"Completely."

I move to rest on my side and look down upon her. "Would you ever have imagined this before you met me again?"

She reaches up to cup my face. "No, but that makes it even better. A kind of surprise that life threw at us. Both doing it this way and the fact that it's with you. And if it works then I get to experience pregnancy all over again."

"For the second time," I point out.

"Everything is better the second time around when it comes to you." She's quick to kiss me, and I can't argue.

BONUS SCENE: REID

I stroke Lena's hair as she lies on her stomach, completely in a state of deep sleep. As much as I want to slide right into her, I know she needs her sleep. She is too beautiful right now, and I could stare at her forever, but I'll leave her in peace.

Stretching my arms, I walk out of our room, close the door gently behind me, then head down the hall of my family's vacation rental into the kitchen to grab a mug of coffee from the pot. With drink in hand, I walk out to the screened porch to enjoy the South Carolina breeze of fresh sea air. Sitting down, I lean back and take in a moment of quiet while letting the coffee hit my lips.

"She's still sleeping?" My mother's voice accompanies her steps.

I don't look up. "Mmhmm. I'll take Oscar to the beach or something so Lena can rest."

My mother sits next to me with a gentle smile fixed on her face. "Oscar went with your father to go pick out new golf equipment at the outlet mall."

I glance to her because, yikes, as much as I love that my

family welcomed Oscar as their own, golf in the sentence just sends a shiver down my spine, as I hate the game.

My folks rented a place in Hilton Head and invited us down, and truthfully, it's been fun. We're only two days in but I'm optimistic.

We both sit in a peaceful silence while my mother taps her fingers against the arm of the rocking chair. "She's pregnant," she states.

I don't look at her and instead try to control the smile that wants to erupt on my lips as I look into my coffee. "I'm not going to get away with saying she's just a little tired, am I?" I look at my mom and her face turns to pure elation. I hold my hand up to stop her. "She doesn't know I know, so please keep this to yourself, which we know how that'll go, but thought I would ask."

"What do you mean you don't know?"

Deep down I know I may just be a mama's boy because I can't not speak with her about it. "I mean, it's obvious, especially when she had to throw up after we collected the rental car. But I know she's waiting to tell me."

"Why?"

I swallow at the pure sentiment of it. "Knowing Lena, she's waiting for the end of the week to share the good news."

My mother grabs my hand to squeeze. "Your cancer-free anniversary. What a great present to give."

I nod in agreement.

"Third time's the charm, right?"

My brows furrow, and I look at her, surprised she knows. It's taken us exactly three tries, with each turkey-baster ceremony getting more emotional as we worked to get to this point.

"Lena may have had a moment when we were at the

grocery store yesterday. She didn't confirm but did admit you've been trying."

"And what did you do?"

"I gave her a hug then said I needed to go find ingredients for my casserole. I gave her space, as I assumed she wanted to buy a test." That was my mother's subtle way of not being overbearing, considering I've never once witnessed my mom cook a casserole.

I purse my lips out before dragging the back of my finger along my upper lip. We sit there in a thick moment of silence.

"She knows you went to the doctor?" she mentions more than asks.

I sigh. "No. I didn't tell her." My eyes sideline to my mom who gives me a look of disapproval.

"Why not?"

"There's nothing to tell. I didn't want to worry her until there was something to worry about. She's been stressed enough with this baby stuff." For my annual check-up, they needed to run an extra test due to some initial results. Turns out it was all a false alarm.

My mother stands and touches my shoulder as she glides past. "Then celebrate."

I hear her greet Lena good morning, and Lena is in my view with a big smile. Grabbing her wrist, I pull her onto my lap.

"Morning. Oscar will be back soon. You feeling okay?" I ask as I pull her hair over one shoulder.

She leans down to kiss me. "Morning. I'm fine, why wouldn't I be?"

I try to play it cool, and I offer her a fake smile. "Okay."

"Was your mother pestering you about when the wedding will happen?" she teases and pinches my arm.

"Nah, we were talking about other stuff." I shrug and take

a moment to look at the ring on her finger of our entwined hands.

Lena studies me as she attempts to interpret what that could mean. "Something you want to tell me?"

"Something you want to tell me?" I counter with a cunning smirk.

She rolls her eyes as she begins to run her hands up my arms to my shoulders. "You figured it out already, huh?"

"Maybe, but it'll be better when I hear you say it."

She inhales a deep breath, with her shoulders hitching up and then down. "Reid, I'm pregnant."

Excellent, she said my name and confirmed the news.

I smile right before I slam my mouth on hers, kissing her in pure joy and the fact it is extremely hot, the idea of watching my baby grow inside of her.

Pulling away, she rubs her thumb along my bottom lip. "I wanted to wait to tell you for your big day."

"I figured, but I like this more. We have two reasons to celebrate this week then."

She combs her fingers through my hair. "Our favorite number in our favorite season."

I scoff a laugh. "Something like that."

I pull her closer and kiss her again, knowing full well that life can't really get better than this.

THANK YOU

Thank you so much for reading! I adored writing Lena and Reid. My favorite season and a romance just made it feel like the warmest cup of hot cocoa on a perfect fall day. I wouldn't be writing without you dear readers. I truly hope this one warmed your heart and made you blush.

Thank you to my editor, Lindsay. I'm running out of things to say because you are my lifeline for every single book that I write.

Sarah from Enchanting Romance Designs, you had the ebook cover before I even wrote. That is pure inspiration! Lily Bear Design also nailed it, as I wasn't even planning on a special design yet it called to me as it is so pretty.

Autumn from Wordsmith Publicity, I should have known being named after my favorite season was a sign that you would be amazing!

Cheryl, for dealing with my chaotic messages and sometimes random organization.

To all the bookstagrammers, TikTokers, bloggers that share- I can't do this without you!

Pumpkin lattes, pumpkin pie, changing leaves, the smell of nutmeg in October, the sounds of Taylor Swift, candles at night, my husband and our small one...thank you for always being there!